AF429223

# Back to Black

## Blackstone, Volume 7

Rachel E Rice

Published by Rachel E Rice, 2024.

Back To Black
A Blackstone Novel
Book 7
By Rachel E Rice
Copyright 2020 by Rachel E Rice

# Table of Contents

Sign up for a newsletter[1] from Rachel E Rice for chapter reveals, free books, and the latest books before they're published. You can contact me at: rachelerice04@gmail.com Thank you for reading my books. Please leave a review. Enjoy! Blog: http://www.rachel-e-rice.com

---

1. http://eepurl.com/4uh-b

# Copyright

Copyright 2020 by Rachel E. Rice

All rights reserved. No part of this book may be used or reproduced in any manner whatsoever without written permission, except in the case of brief quotations embodied in critical articles or reviews. Please do not participate in or encourage the piracy of copyrighted materials in violation of the author's rights. Purchase only authorized editions.

This is a work of fiction. Names, characters, places, and incidents are the product of the author's imagination. Any resemblance to actual persons, living or dead, events, or locales is entirely coincidental. No reproduction of this book part or whole is permitted. This book should not be scanned, or distributed in any printed or electronic form without the author's permission.

<h1 style="text-align:right">Chapter 1</h1>

Max didn't want to leave Alex lying in the bed, but he had to go. He turned and gazed at her beautiful body with its smooth flawless skin. Something stirred inside of him whenever he looked on her lying there with the covers drawn back. He leaned over down, kissed her buttocks, then trailed his lips to her back, pushed her hair gently aside and nipped at her neck.

Alex stirred and gave out a soft moan of pleasure as she laid nude beside him with his thoughts of last night rushing through his head.

He thought about how she'd turned and laid on her stomach when he'd fucked her from behind, his favorite fantasy position when she'd called him Master. She even wore a blindfold and allowed him to use his black ribbons to tie her hands, but not her ankles. She'd laid on her stomach first, then up on her knees as she took the position of submissive whenever he'd have to say goodbye to her. It was becoming more and more difficult to leave as each day past.

Alex became his submissive to reinforce his mindset whenever he had to deal with men where he'd have to make important decisions and tonight would be one of those times.

Knowing what Max needed mentally had become her new job. His mind set had been very important when making decisions about his many companies, and she worked with him to reinforce his Alpha status especially in the bedroom.

The bedroom had been where it had been most important for them to maintain a healthy marriage. Their sex life had been the center of their success as a married couple because Max had to be away because of his position as owner of the Blackstone companies. There was no one left in the Blackstone family to run the company, well almost no one but Jonas, and Max wouldn't trust Jonas to go around the corner.

When Max had made love to Alex earlier that night, when she'd been lying on her back, legs splayed waiting for him to take her, Max crawled between her legs, sucking her clit, bringing her to orgasm, and she'd moaned, "When you make love to me, Max, my joy is surrendering to you." She'd cup his face with her fingers, and he'd kiss her hard, their tongues entwined, he'd suck it down, at the same time burying his cock deep inside her opening.

In the bedroom, as the Master to Alex's Submissive, Max found his strength to leave Alex because he'd never wanted to. He could be happy for the rest of his life with his family and inside Alex's body day and night.

Max placed his hands between her legs, and with his finger he'd pushed in and pulled out of her pussy, smelled her arousing scent which had his cock throbbing. She'd respond each time and let him satisfy himself in whatever fashion he wanted because she belonged to him and he belonged to her.

Alex had worn his collar signaling that she'd been his slave in the bedroom—a thin platinum necklace with a heart and key that said *mine* on the back of the heart, and underneath *mine*, it read—if found, *return to Maximillian Blackstone.*

Max wore his collar, but not tonight. It had studs and was bulky, and had been placed in a drawer in their playroom to be worn when he'd returned to Alex from one of his never ending business trips.

• • • •

"WHY ARE YOU STILL HERE? I thought after you hid those bodies, got my wife involved with your craziness, you'd leave, and head back to wherever the fuck you go when you can't deal with life. Alex hasn't gotten over that last shit you had her mixed up in. She gets nightmares and you're the blame for that," Max barked.

"You mean she isn't tying you up and flogging you the way you like her too." Max reached for a glass and threw it at the cabinet.

"Damn you, Jonas. You've been nothing but a distraction for Alex and a reminder of all that shit in New York." Jonas turned to face Max.

"Alex wants me here. Ask her. She'll tell you."

"I want you gone. This is my house and I need you to fucking leave soon."

"I've never heard you use those words to me before."

"What the word *fuck*? Then get used to it."

"No. The words where you tell me you don't want me around your family anymore. It's just me and you left. We are all that remains of our family."

"Look around. I have a family, and you, where is your wife and children?" Max walked to the foyer and called Alex's name. When he didn't hear anyone, he marched back to where Jonas sat in a leather chair peering out of the window.

"Where's Alex and the kids?" Max marched up to where Jonas sat and glanced over at Jonas, then aiming his eyes in the same direction, watching what Jonas appeared to be looking at— the snow and a doe and a fawn.

Max had dropped his satchel, sauntered through broken glass, reached for a glass in the cabinet of the large room to pour himself a drink. "What have you been doing all day? Don't you think you should get to Seattle and see your wife and children?"

"I have no wife, only children. Crystal left me," Jonas replied. Max furrowed his brow and drank his Scotch without ice. He held on to the empty glass and sat on the sofa across from where Jonas sat. Jonas never met his eyes, he kept looking out at the fallen snow. "How can you live out here?"

"Easily. You should try it." It was the sound of Max's voice that made Jonas shift his body to face him.

"Did I do something? You've been unforgiving and offensive since you walked in here. "

"The question should be, when have you done anything that wasn't destructive to yourself and Alex and to my family. I almost lost Alex last time. My children had no mother for months. How could you of all people ask me what have you done? Where do you want me to start?"

Jonas stood, his jaw tightened, he glared at Max, and Max never turned away. "Don't make me the fall guy. You're as much to blame as anyone." Max turned his face away. "What is it, Max? Say it. Tell me how you feel about me once and for all." Max rose from the chair and headed to the cabinet where he'd moments earlier poured a drink. He reached for a bottle where he kept his Scotch. The bottle emptied by him a minute before.

Max reached and unscrewed the bottle and poured more liquor into the same glass and then put it to his lips, and drank it until it was empty. Then he glanced over where his twin brother sat and with all the courage it would take he said, "I want you to leave, tomorrow."

That must have caught Jonas by surprise because he sprang from his seat. "Where the fuck do you want me to go?"

"I don't care, Jonas, I don't give a fuck where you go. You're grown. When you wanted to open those clubs you didn't consult me."

"You know why I did that. No one would hire me after I got out of the service, not even a seven eleven. I was too nervous and had all these pills the VA doctors forced on me. They said if I didn't take them I could never function as a man. I could never have a life, so I took them and those same pills made me worse. It was those fucking pills which had me hallucinating and addicted to them."

I open those bondage clubs because it gave me peace. Those clubs were good enough for you because of your sleeping problems. It was because of me that you have Alex. I see it served its purpose. I served my purpose and now you want me gone out of your life. So you don't have to be reminded of your complicity in all of this. When Alex serves her purpose, will you kick her out too?"

"Don't you fucking bring Alex in this or drag me in," Max roared.

"You've done enough on your end. It wasn't me who hired that freak Robert to watch her." Max walked close to Jonas, his eyes blistering with anger as they narrowed, and his jaw tightened. Jonas knew that look and he stepped away from Max, and Max poured himself another drink.

Now he was calm and he could tell his brother what he needed to say. "You have to go Jonas because I don't want you around my children."

"You mean you don't want me around Alex."

"Whatever the fuck way you want to put it. You need to leave. When I return, I don't want you here." Max practiced those words a hundred times, he didn't think he could ever say them to Jonas, but he did, and it took three glass of Scotch without ice to get those words out. Inside Max's heart filled with pain, but he knew he had to get it out. He had to get Jonas away from Alex before something worse happens.

It was the hardest thing he'd ever done. Jonas was his younger brother and identical twin. If it hurt him it must have been like a hammer crushing Max's heart too.

Jonas turned like a zombie, stiff, and walked back to the chair facing the floor to ceiling windows. He stood against the frosted glass watched the snow fall and the deer running aimlessly in the yard.

"I'm sorry, Jonas. There was no other way for me to say this." He placed his palm on Jonas's shoulder and he felt Jonas tremble. Jonas turned to face Max without an expression. Max didn't need to read Jonas's face. He read his body language, and he knew Jonas's mind.

"Did you tell Alex and the children?" Jonas's voice low and subdued.

"No. I'm leaving that for you because I have to shower and dress and leave again. I thought my family would be here."

Jonas with his blue eyes stared into Max's face. It was like looking into a mirror. The only difference had been the clothes. Max wore black suits and white shirts. Jonas, when he wasn't imitating Max, wore black shirts, black leather coats, and black jeans.

"Didn't you promise Alex that you'd cut back on your traveling. I told you I could help out." In his own way Jonas couldn't bring himself to accept what Max wanted. However, he had little choice now.

"I don't want you to help out. Can't you see that? I don't want you replacing me. You've done enough damage as it were. I can't send you to meetings in my place because since you've come from New York, and all that shit that occurred there, you've acted as if you've lost it. I'm afraid that you'll say something, or heaven forbid do something once again to put my entire family in jeopardy."

"I'll never say anything to anyone." Jonas glanced up at Max as if he was still that little boy who Max had to tell that their parents and all their immediate family had died in a plane crash. After Jonas came back from Afghanistan, he was never the same. He came back with all his limbs, but his mind wasn't quite right.

"Look, Jonas. This is the hardest thing I have to do, but I can't let you destroy my wife and my family. You've done enough damage. And I've done enough trying to clean up behind you everywhere you've gone. I don't want to discover that you've gotten my wife into any more of your sordid shit. We have children."

"I won't do that again. I've learned my lesson, Max. Please give me another chance," Jonas pleaded.

"I've given you all the chances I can give and you've cost everyone more than you will ever be able to pay back." Max picked up his satchel and trudged out of the room leaving a broken Jonas with his head low. He hadn't had a drink in over a year, but he needed one now. He needed to think about what he'd do next.

Jonas pulled his coat and hat from the closet and placed on a pair of boots, and after the boots were secured, Jonas shrugged his arms through his warm coat. He'd go for a walk. Maybe when he'd have enough time to think, he'd come up with a solution. He sauntered out the door to the back of the house, passed by the servants quarters, and then down a trail that he'd used many times before, but never in this kind of blistering cold weather.

The snow was falling, Jonas raised his face, closed his eyes, walked, and walked. Through the trees, in a circle and then back to the lights of the large home he lived in with his brother, Alex, and their children. It had gotten dark now when he came in and went straight to his room on the other side of the house.

He didn't see why he had to leave. He didn't take up much space, he'd been there to keep Alex company, and to protect her. Max had been hardly ever home when he swore to Alex that he would be. But Jonas had always been there helping out with the children. Taking them to school, to soccer, skiing, and skating practice. He even bought horses for them to ride with him in the summer.

Just what the fuck did Max expect him to do? He wondered, after entering his room and lying on the bed, Jonas fell asleep, when he woke the house was dark except for his room where he began packing to leave.

"I'm leaving, Alex." Alexander Blackstone turned, faced the right side of the bed where Max had slept each night whenever he was home, and not on a flight out of the country, or when they found that they needed rest more than they needed the assurance of being inside each other's bodies.

Her hands reached for her eyes wiping away the deep sleep and blurred vision from being awakened in the middle of a dream. The dream that she'd been safe and at home in Maximillian's arms, their children resting in the rooms down the hall.

Blinking to focus on the handsome sexy figure standing before her, she couldn't understand why Max had been wearing jeans and a leather jacket, and not his usual attire a dark suit, white shirt, whenever he traveled.

Max always flew on his private jet dressed in a black suit and white shirt with his ties in his satchel to use when the occasion called for him to wear one which was most of the time. But why was he dressed in casual clothes? It was too late or too early for her brain to work so she didn't think about it. She sighed as she did when Max would leave, and she'd turn on her back for him to kiss her.

As the figure leaned over her, she placed her palm through the open shirt and felt Max's hard chest or so she thought.

Alex relaxed only when she knew Max had returned to her, but he wasn't returning, he was leaving, and she felt an emptiness that had accompanied his departures. He'd said that he would stay home more, but he hadn't kept his promise. She'd forgive him this once since he'd been through so much with her lately taking the attention away from their children.

Narrowing her gaze, still not quite awake, she whispered in a throaty sexy voice as she massaged and raked her fingers through the fine dark hairs of his muscular chest. "Give me a kiss," she whispered.

Her eyes hadn't adjusted to the darkened room. "You know where I want it before you go," she murmured with closed eyes pulling the covers down to reveal her thighs.

She felt the bed dip next to her.

"I'm leaving. I thought you should know."

"What do you mean you're leaving? I thought you were supposed to leave last night," she said finally comprehending what he'd said. "Where did you sleep? In the basement again?" Alex questioned. "Not in the basement, Max? You promised me. You spend too much time in that basement. I thought you wouldn't sleep there overnight without telling me. You know I miss you when you're not near me. I was in the middle of this dream." She smiled.

Alex reached for his hand, he leaned in to kiss her, and she placed her palm on his face rubbing it over his stubble.

"You haven't shaved. That's not like you. What are you worried about this time? No, don't tell me. I thought you said you would sell off all those overseas holdings."

Alex placed her finger over his mouth stopping the few words from falling from his lips. "I know, you never worry. You just handle it. Give me a kiss before you go," Alex uttered, still trying to navigate the dim lit room, feeling tired from running around all day shopping with her children, and making love to Max almost every night since she'd returned from that harrowing kidnapping experience in New York.

Wondering how Max could keep up the pace of traveling, seeing to her, she couldn't fathom where he'd gotten his energy. He had meetings in different cities, flying home at night, making love to her, then flying out again, and this time to Hong Kong. She didn't want him to go for obvious reasons, but there was no way to stop him.

Maximillian Blackstone was a singled minded man who appeared to be in control of everything. However, Alex knew the true Maximillian Blackstone like no one ever could, or ever will, and still she didn't know him fully or completely.

Who does know anyone that well?

His twin brother Jonas Blackstone was another animal entirely. He and Max identical twins, Alex knew Jonas better than any man she'd met, even Max. Jonas was the opposite of Max. Jonas wasn't as outgoing or confident unless he was posing as Max, which he did quite often, and most of the time at Max's insistence and to his determent.

Max had enlisted his wayward brother to represent him on more than one occasion, especially when he didn't want to sit in on a meeting. And that's where Jonas shined. He out Maxed Max. If he'd been graded on his impersonation he'd gotten an A and Max a B for being himself.

Jonas had never been secure in his own skin and Alex knew that. She knew him too well. He was more at home pretending to be Maximillian Blackstone instead of Jonas Blackstone the army veteran, a man so damaged, and so fucked up that he knew how dangerous he'd been to Alex and his brother.

Alex wrapped her arms around that handsome man's neck, the man she thought to be her husband, and met his warm lips with a soft kiss, which caused him to capture her lips with his, and what was supposed to be a friendly goodbye kiss from Jonas, became something much more—heated and blistering. A kiss that could sear a woman's soul.

Before his tongue entered her parted lips, Alex pulled away. "I need to brush my teeth if this is what I think it is."

"I don't care and he aimed his tongue into her open mouth.

Her eyes opened wide, as she sucked his tongue because the hard heated kiss had felt different from the one Max had often offered her lately on leaving. Max's kisses had been quick and smooth. This one was much more.

Startled, Alex pulled back. Sitting up, then leaning reaching for the nearby lamp to turn it on, she stammered, "What? What are you doing in my room, Jonas? You know you shouldn't be here. Where's Max?"

Alex frowned and her smooth brow furrowed. She felt repulsed and then she relaxed.

"I think Max left last night for the airport. I came to tell you that I'm leaving." Alex sat breathing hard and calming down.

"Why didn't you tell me it was you?"

"I thought you knew," Jonas insisted.

"You thought you could kiss me that way and I would want and approve of you doing this? You are wrong Jonas. I don't love you that way. I never could so get that out of your sick mind."

Jonas lowered his head, looked wide eyed like a fearful child after getting a scolding from his mother for stealing money for candy. "I'm sorry, Alex. Please don't tell Max."

"I would never do anything like that. I know you didn't mean to do it. I blame myself more than you. I should have known the difference in you and Max. Not only that, if I've done anything to make you think that I would betray Max with you, then it's my fault."

"You've never done anything and I've over stepped my bounds. It's me. I fell in love with you and I shouldn't have. It's my own stupidity and need."

Jonas's head rose and the shame remained in his eyes. When he stood tall once again, his eyes couldn't meet Alex's. The weight and the fear of Max finding out what he'd done would be lifted from his shoulders after Alex assured him that Max would never find out.

When Alex reached for his hand he knew that they could put this lapse of judgment behind them. Jonas took a deep breath and lifted his head and shoulders.

After Alex recovered from the initial shock of Jonas kissing her, she questioned him, "Going where? Where are you going, Jonas? You know you don't do well without Max telling you what to do. I thought you were going to see Crystal and your children before you made a decision to leave here. You said that you would try for a reconciliation. You know she loves you."

"I love her, too, but it's obvious that we can't live together, or maybe it's me who can't get it together where someone would want to be with me for more than a day or a month."

"Why are you beating yourself up Jonas? We love you. Max and I love you." He turned and gave Alex a hesitant smile.

"I know you love me, Alex, in your own way, and so does Max, but as far as Crystal is concerned it's over. I'm the father of our children and that's where it ends. Too much have happened for me to even pretend that I'm a sane man anymore. The army, New York. I can't forget that even if you can. You're good for compartmentalizing, Alex. I wish I could be like you and Max.

"I didn't want to tell you, Alex, but Crystal found someone else. She and the children are better off without me. That's what Max said." Jonas once again had a forlorn look in his eyes. He had a habit of staring and thinking. Alex had noticed that Jonas had been partial to staring blankly, and each time he did that she'd called it to his attention, and suggested that he see a therapist that could help him. He'd taken her advice and that hadn't happened for some time, until now.

He snapped out of it in a few seconds.

Jonas had admitted to Alex that these were the side effects of drugs, and had something to do with the meds he'd been on since he'd had his breakdown after returning home from Afghanistan.

"Everyone is better off without me. I have a way of fucking up everything I touch. Look at all the shit I caused in New York. All the people who died because of me. And I managed to get you into all kinds of shit."

"That wasn't all your fault. But things have a way of getting fucked up whenever you're around. I must admit," Alex joked and smiled. Jonas sat when Alex pulled him close. Then she raked her fingers through Jonas's curls when he sat near her. Then Alex took Jonas's face in her hands.

"Jonas Blackstone, you are the kindest, outrageous, handsome, and one of the best men I've met and that includes your brother whom I love with a passion. If I wasn't married to Max, you would have been my first choice, if I hadn't met Max before you. But then if I hadn't met Max when I did, I never would have had the pleasure of your love. We've been through a lot together. You and I have a bond that can never be broken. Not the same as Max and I, but an unspeakable bond that unites us in ways no one can understand but us."

Alex placed her palms on both sides of his stubble, handsome face, smiled, leaned in, and gave Jonas a brief soft kiss on his lips.

Their eyes locked. "If you ever need me... I know I shouldn't say that after New York, but I have to. You have your family here with us, and I belong to that family even if I'm the wife. If you ever need me, call me, Jonas," Alex whispered into Jonas's mouth, and pulled her lips away.

"You can't lead me on, or lie to me, Alex. I know what you're doing. You and I know that there is no one like my brother, and there can be no one else but him for you. Even if you'd met me first, then when he came along, you would have left me to be with him."

Alex's brown eyes brightened and a gigantic smile crossed her lips. What Jonas had said was the truth, and he knew Alex was trying to make him feel better about himself.

"Where are you going, Jonas? I need to know. Someone should know. Have you contacted your doctors?"

Jonas never answered, he rose attempting to head for the door after giving Alex one last closed smile, but Alex placed her hand on his wrist and gave it a tug. "Don't go far and call or text. Maybe even face time with me. When you get where you're going, I'd like to know if you're okay, and where you decided to move to."

"I'm thinking about Florida. Hitchhike to Miami. Maybe take a bus and see how the other half lives."

"I know how the other half lives and I would caution against it. Why don't you take one of the cars? You will need it where you're going," Alex cautioned.

"I have money to buy a car if I wanted, more money than I will ever spend, or need. Max placed money in my account. He still thinks if he gives me all my inheritance that I'll blow it on a pretty woman." Jonas aimed a wide smile at Alex. She knew that Max knew Jonas almost as well as she did." Max had to get Jonas out of more trouble involving women than either one of them cared to think about.

"I let my license expire," Jonas said, placing his hands in his jean pockets when he was nervous and didn't want to answer any more questions. Alex knew that Jonas hadn't let his license expire. That was just to placate her, and he would do as he set out to do no matter what Max had said, or what she warned him not to do.

It was time she stopped coddling him, she thought, and let Jonas be Jonas.

Now that was a scary thought.

"Do you think Florida is a good place to move to since it's not far from New York?" Alex questioned, not wanting to say goodbye where she felt this time she wouldn't see him again.

"It's far enough. It's crowded and I can get lost there. I've been to San Francisco and made a mess out there, too. I've just about made a mess everywhere I've gone. I'm getting older now. If I can't be marriage material, then maybe I can be a good father, or at least slow down and try."

Jonas's mouth tightened and he bit his bottom lip and his eyes wandered.

"The therapy appears to be working and with the meds I'm on, I think I'm stabilized. We'll see."

"You'll make it, Jonas. You'll be fine. I have faith in you."

"You might be the only one. Max has given up on me. Don't give up on me, Alex. You're all I have."

"We are your family. My children and Max and I. You will always have us." Jonas took a few steps and leaned over, and kissed Alex on the forehead as if he couldn't leave, afraid to make that step that would take him out of the security of Max's home.

Pulling away, Jonas stared down at Alex and held on to her hand as if it was connected to his. He didn't want to let go. Maybe he thought that if he did, it would sever the ties and dissolve the feelings Alex had for him. Forever. He would never forget her, and how they'd bonded because of their crazy love-hate-love relationship.

His love for her, and her hate for the things she offered to do for him in the name of love.

The weather had been ruthless all day and night with the wind rain and snow, but now that Jonas was leaving Montana, it still didn't let up with the wind and snow. Jonas knew driving had been out of the question anyway, and since there was a local bus station in the nearby town he opted to take the bus.

Alex's driver dropped him at the bus station inside a local store.

After buying a ticket to Miami, Jonas boarded, placed his backpack overhead and settled back in his seat to watch a movie. No doubt that he would watch many before the bus pulled into Miami. The seat next to him had been empty, and he thought that he'd be able to relax without having to talk to anyone.

He didn't like small talk, the usual about the weather, and his name. Maximillian had made a name for himself with all the land he owned and the ski resorts. If you were traveling through Montana you'd see that Blackstone name imprinted everywhere.

Just when the bus was due to take off, and Jonas sucked in a sigh of relief, a man wearing jeans, Goose-down coat came running, spotted the only empty seat left, and plopped down next to Jonas.

After the man sat down in his coat and scarf, he introduced himself, looked around and proudly stated that he was going to Florida. After relaxing the man turned to Jonas, "Where you going in Florida?" the man with the heavy coat and boots questioned Jonas after looking him up and down searching for a friendly face. Jonas didn't give him what he'd hoped for. Jonas wasn't friendly and neither was he distant. He just wanted quiet and peace.

"We have a long way to go. Just trying to make a friend before we travel over two thousand miles. It's better to be friends because that's a long way to be this close and not talk." He extended his hand to Jonas. "Names Grayland."

Jonas took his hand with a hard handshake. "That's some kind of handshake you've got there." Jonas looked him over. When the man with the brownish thick hair shrugged off his coat and then hat, Jonas glanced at him. He had been smaller than Jonas thought, nevertheless, he had wide shoulders. Kind of stocky and tall. Maybe six feet. "You don't talk much do you?"

"Not much. The names Jonas." He extended his hand in hopes that would be the end of the conversation. Jonas turned to look out at the passing scenery.

But like the man said, two thousand miles was a long way not to talk to anyone, especially someone so close.

After a thousand miles and stops at more bus stations than he could count, Jonas reevaluated his idea to travel by bus. He'd made up his mind quick as he'd been known to do and followed his mind.

"I'm getting off at the next stop. The man turned to him, "Is it something I did?"

"No you were what I called a sterling passenger. When I didn't want to talk you didn't. You respected my wishes and my space. I just don't think that this kind of travel is for me. I... I should go to the local car dealership and buy a car."

"You can do that? Just buy yourself a car, pay cash?"

"Yes. Do you know the name...Blackstone?" Jonas didn't know if he should use his last name, but the guy put up with him and gave his full name. He thought the neighborly thing to do was to tell him his. Jonas had never been neighborly, he'd just been a loner. *Maybe a change would do him some good,* he thought.

"You're not telling me that your name is Blackstone. The Blackstone. I'm Jonas Blackstone and the name you saw plastered on buildings from the west coast to the east coast that has the Blackstone name is because of my brother Maximillian."

"But just because he's rich doesn't make you rich."

"I'm not as rich as Max, but I can buy a new car if I want. Do you care to take a ride with me?"

"Fuck yeah, if you let me help you drive."

"Sure. I was hoping you said that. Since we're going to Miami, what kind of car do you think I should get?" Jonas questioned.

"You're asking me?"

"Why not?" Jonas laughed.

"What about a convertible? I've always fancied driving a convertible corvette?"

"Let's go get that yellow corvette." When the bus stopped at the next station the two friends climbed off the bus and in less time it took for paperwork, Jonas had a yellow corvette headed for Miami, Florida.

"I never knew people who could buy a car just like that. My family worked our horse ranch and barely had enough money left over after breaking horses to buy a car with all the money between us." Grayland turned to Jonas, "What are you planning on doing once you get to Miami?"

"Just lie on the beach and chill. Maybe open a bar after I get bored sitting around. And you, what are your plans?"

"Get myself a job of some kind. Anything is better than doing what I've been doing. I've broken my back, legs, and arms. That weather in Montana just about killed me. If the horses didn't the weather would, so I packed it in and told my mother that I'd rather die in the sun than get broken up by a horse, and have her to take care of me." Jonas glanced over at Grayland.

"When I'm ready, what do you say you come and work for me?"

"Do you know anything about bars?" Jonas asked.

"Only that I can drink anyone under the table on a Saturday night."

"Well, you're hired my friend. At least you can recognize when someone has had too much to drink," Jonas chuckled. Grayland made Jonas laugh, and that had been in short supply lately.

"Are you serious, Jonas?"

"Don't I look like a serious man?"

"Sometimes," Grayland said, raising an eyebrow and smiling.

As Grayland drove into Miami, Jonas glanced over and asked, "Where are you staying?"

"I have a sister. She left the ranch to go to college and never came back. She's my older sister."

"And you're how old, Grayland?"

"Twenty-five. My sister is forty-five. That makes her too old for you. And she has a husband."

"Well the age doesn't put me off, it's the husband." The two had a laugh and before they drove up to Grayland's sister's house, they exchanged phone numbers. "I'll text you if you haven't found work, and maybe you can manage my bar for me."

"Is that a promise, Jonas?"

"A promise. I'll be in touch." Jonas helped Grayland take out his two pieces of luggage from the corvette, they smiled, and shook hands before Grayland brought Jonas in for a hug. "I'll be seeing you, my friend," Jonas said clearing his throat. Jonas had never had a friend before. Only Max his brother and Alex. Max was more of a brother than a friend. Max watched over him and told him when he'd fucked up which was all the time. That wasn't a friend's job. He considered Alex a friend because she never judged him. Max was more of a protector. He'd protected Jonas since he'd gotten out of the army and proceeded to get into all kinds of trouble.

Jonas only had the men in his platoon who were friends and brothers. They watched each other's back the way Max watched over Jonas, but there were only two men left out of his sixteen band of brother's when their deployment was up.

He'd lost touch with the other man.

After stepping into his corvette, he turned to see Grayland ringing the bell and then a woman in her early forties, or who he thought was Grayland's sister, opened the door and gave him a big hug before ruffling his hair like Grayland was a little boy.

When they disappeared into the house, Jonas turned on the motor and zoomed off into the direction of the beach. He'd rented a house on the beach before he'd left Montana, but never revealed that to Alex for fear she'd tell Max. He wanted to stay off the grid for a while and then when he'd settled down, he'd let them know where he lived. Maybe have them up to visit with the children.

That was his plans, but as the adage goes, *the best laid plans of mice and men tend to go astray.*

Pulling into the driveway of his newly rented home, he glanced around, heard the ocean waves as his corvette came to a stop in front of this beautiful one story place. It appeared larger than he'd wanted and now he had to hire someone to clean it which he didn't want to do, but it became necessary when he entered and saw that it was enormous and there was no way he could manage the place alone.

Jonas didn't bother to ask about the square footage, he didn't know or cared at the time about things like that, he just wanted to get away, and get as far away from Maximillian. He had a lot to prove to Max and Alex, and there was no better place or time than to do it in Miami.

After taking his backpack out of the car, he did a walk-through of the house to see where everything was.

The fridge was empty and he had to get some groceries. He'd been tired and searched his phone for a Pizza delivery and found it. But in the meantime it would be Pizza and cola. Jonas hadn't drank liquor in a year, and he wasn't about to break his months of sobriety. He'd sworn off alcohol.

When he mentioned to Max that he'd be leaving and had plans to open a bar, Max warned him about being around liquor.

"You haven't been free of all that shit that went on at your Bondage Club and now you want to open a bar? Are you out of your fucking mind, Jonas?" Those words were bitter in his ear and worked to fuck up his mind, but he'd been determined to prove Max wrong.

"You of all people, Max, should have some confidence in me. I've gotten in trouble not because I drank, but because I opened those bondage clubs. I can't see how that should have affected you?"

"It affected me because you got Alex involved in your fucking shit. I could have lost her because of you. I don't blame her I blame you. She was only trying to help my poor confused brother."

"I'm not confused, Max. I know what I want to do. I have to make a place for myself and I can't do that with you cleaning up behind me."

"For fuck's sake, Jonas, I have always cleaned up your mess. I can't have a life because of you. I have a family and what did you do? You had a chance with Crystal and your child, but you fucked that up by getting into all kinds of shit in New York. Do you know what I had to do to get you out of that mess? Do you realize I could have lost the mother of my children with your criminal behavior?"

"I didn't set out to do this. I know I've done somethings in my life, but I never killed anyone except in war."

"You never killed anyone? Then why did you enlist in the army and reenlist. You had money you weren't like the other men in your platoon who got themselves killed because they didn't have another choice. You had everything, and you managed to fuck that up, and that's why I want you to leave before you fuck up my family."

Those were the last bitter words coming from Max's mouth last week. Jonas felt as if Max had been in this house with him.

Jonas plopped down on the sofa and flicked on the large television hanging over the fireplace. *What the fuck do they need a fireplace in Miami for anyway?* He thought. Jonas chuckled. This had been the second laugh he'd had in a long time. Just as he flicked the channel and kicked off his shoes, the bell rang.

He opened the door to see a young blond man, eighteen or nineteen, standing holding a pizza box and a large bottle of cola.

Pulling the money out of his jeans, he handed him a generous tip along with the price of the pizza and coke. When the teen thanked him and turned to walk away, Jonas asked, "Do you live around here?"

"In the area but not these homes. My family can't afford the rent."

"Do you know the name of the nearest supermarket that delivers?"

"Sure." He wrote the name of the market for Jonas. Then the delivery guy said, "This is a lot of home for one man. Are you expecting your family?"

"I'm single."

"Oh, a bachelor. Dude you're in the right place. The beach is crawling with beautiful women looking for a handsome dude with money."

"I'm not looking for anything or anyone. I came here to rest."

"Well good luck." Jonas dismissed what the guy said, and carried the pizza and cola to the kitchen, ate his pizza and watched the sports channel until he fell asleep. It had been the first time he'd slept this peacefully in months. Maybe even a year.

For some reason he couldn't sleep at Max and Alex's place. Maybe it was the children and all the animals around that had him anxious. Maybe it was Max with his judgmental eyes and words that made him uneasy all the time.

He no longer had to look at Max, but he wished he could see Alex. Maybe facetime with her and the children, he thought.

When Jonas woke it was to a loud scream, "What the fuck?" He said and dashed through the house, through the patio doors, and into the garden to see a man arguing with a young woman.

Jonas peered over a hedge and got a clear view of a young beautiful woman about twenty-five with long dark hair. The man she'd appeared to be arguing with had to be in his late thirties or forty. Jonas couldn't be sure in that dim light. The forty-something man had been attractive with grey on the sides of his temples that Jonas could see.

He could see that the man had the pretty woman by her arms shaking her. Jonas didn't know what to do, but he'd learned to mind his own business unless the man was trying to harm her, but it didn't look like that was the case with the two of them.

When the argument died down, Jonas headed for the house and into the bedroom for a shower. After his shower he listened for noise, but there were none so he fell across the California King bed and slept until the sun peeked through the shutters.

After coffee Jonas dressed and went for a walk on the beach. When he looked in front of him he was coming face to face with the same woman he'd seen across the hedge. As she neared him, she smiled and then stopped. He kept walking.

"Thank you."

Jonas stopped, turned, and said, "Were you talking to me?"

"Yes." They were facing each other and Jonas could see that she was a stunning dark haired beauty, and much younger than he thought. She had to be no more than eighteen but she looked at a glance as if she was twenty.

"Did you have a problem with your father last night?"

"He's not my father. He's my lover."

"Oh. I'm sorry." And Jonas started to walk away.

"Don't be sorry. I saw you staring at us and was glad that you didn't intervene. I didn't mean for it to get out of hand, but sometimes he wants me to do things that I don't feel like doing."

"I know what you mean." Jonas was just being polite. He didn't want to know exactly what it was she didn't want to participate in. He'd been around and he'd known the signs and saw them. A young woman and older man. The woman getting involved with a man because of his money. And he looked as if he had enough to command her attention.

This man had to be like Jonas, although the woman didn't know the kind of man Jonas was. He was handsome and rich. However, Jonas wasn't as old as the man, and he didn't have this beautiful woman to call his own and in that way Jonas envied that man.

"Do you really know what I mean?" She glared at Jonas with amber eyes, flicked her dark silky long hair to the side. "Care to go for a swim."

"Not now. I'm not dressed for an early morning swim."

"I didn't mean now. Tonight. What about tonight? My name is Brooke, and yours?" Jonas paused before he would give his name.

"Jonas."

Brooke inched closer to him. "Jonas. That's it?"

"I don't like to give my surname."

"You're not a fugitive are you?"

"No. I don't think so. I haven't had time to check." Brooke chuckled.

"I like you. You make me laugh. So will you swim with me tonight? Should I say skinny dip?"

"Won't your boyfriend mind?"

"He'll be busy tonight."

"What time?"

"Nine o'clock is good," Brooke said.

"Then nine it is." Jonas and Brooke stared at each other for a moment and a smiled crossed their faces at the same time. Then Jonas turned to jog away and for some unsuspecting reason he shouted, "You're beautiful." He knew nothing about this woman, but she captivated him. Was it her youth, not really, because he had many young women before her. Maybe it was her apparent innocence combined with a boldness. Or maybe she'd reminded him of someone he'd loved dearly.

Jonas trotted away, proud and confident, anticipating what tonight would bring.

Time wasn't passing fast enough so Jonas decided to get some chores done. He needed clothes for the warm weather and he needed groceries. Instead of getting them delivered he decided to go to the market.

On leaving the market, he passed a strip mall and there on the outside, a large sign: **For Sale or Rent.** Jonas drove into the mall and looked around. It was just what he needed. Large enough for a club. Not the kind he once had, but more of a bar that served drinks and maybe food. He wrote down the number and called from his car.

"I'm inquiring about the property at this strip mall. It says for sale or rent."

"I'm the owner's secretary and I manage some of his properties. Let me see." She paused a moment as if she was checking which one Jonas wanted. "The property belongs to Mr. Cartwright and it's not for rent. He'd like to see the whole complex sold if you're interested?"

"I have to get back to you." And Jonas hung up. He had to think about it. Was he going to be in Miami long? It all depended on Brooke. He'd been attracted to her the minute he saw her standing almost nude with her boyfriend.

After returning home, he had time to consider whether he'd purchase the property or not, on his drive along the beach highway. However, he needed some extra money. The money he'd gotten from Max had to go only so far, and it didn't include making any more investments. He had to leave his club in New York because it had been overtaken by some shady characters, like the lawyers he'd hired to go over his books and receipts. They'd failed to pay the taxes and everyone who could get a piece of his Bondage club after the IRS got their portion, got more than their share.

Jonas never thought anything over and it appeared he never learned his lesson. He called the only person who he thought could help him. This time he wasn't asking Alex for her help after she and Max got him out of the last shit-storm he gotten Alex and himself in. This time it would be different. He just needed a little advance because he knew he could make the bar profitable. It was small enough for him to control, and he could lease out the remainder of the property.

Jonas scrolled through his phone looking for Alex's number and hit the green button.

"Alex, can you talk?"

"Oh Jonas. I was thinking about you. I miss you and the children miss you."

"What about Max. Does he miss me?"

"He loves you Jonas."

"That's not what I asked. Does Max miss me?" There was a long silence.

"I guess you answered my questioned. I called because you're the one person who never let me down and believed in me." Another long pause as Alex wondered what Jonas was ready to ask her and she'd been ready to tell him no. But could she ever tell him no?

"I need some money."

"Sure, Jonas, how much do you need?" She'd failed that test.

"I don't know but you can't tell Max."

"I said that I would never do what I'd done before. You of all people know just how destructive it was to hide things from him."

"You don't have to hide from Max, just don't tell him. Don't you have money?"

"I'd almost forgotten I'd received money from my mother after her death. Yes, I do."

"Would you consider lending me something? I don't know how much it is until I speak to the owner, but I want to buy some property here in Miami Beach. I can't go on asking Max and have him scrutinize everything I do. I'm thirty-five fucking years old. And Max is a controlling fuck. You know that Alex."

Alex did know, and that's why she empathized with Jonas. "I'll lend it to you."

"Don't worry, Alex, you'll get it back with dividends."

"I'm not worried, Jonas. I just worry about my family and you're part of that family. I don't want anything to happen to you. I need you to be alive and happy. Then I'm happy."

"Another thing, Alex. I met someone. Her name is Brooke. I'll fill you in on it, but right now I have a date to meet her on the beach. Call you tomorrow and tell you all about her and tell you when and where you can wire the money."

When Jonas hit the red button, he glanced at his phone looking at the time. *It's time to meet Brooke,* he thought. He'd never been this anxious before. His heart raced and hammered in his chest. Brooke wasn't his type. Young, maybe twenty but he doubted it, inexperienced or so he thought.

Jonas quickly shrugged on a white tee with a pair of cargo shorts, and wore nothing underneath. They were going for a swim in the nude, why the fuck would he need to wear his boxers? That would only take up more time dressing and undressing. He had plans when he called the nearest restaurant and pre-ordered food. He didn't know what she ate but he knew she didn't eat much. Maybe sushi so he ordered that and a steak for him. To be safe, he let the chef decide on another dish. Jonas had asked for expert help. "What would a young woman eat if she were to go to their restaurant?"

The manager said that he'd send something extra with Jonas's order and considering the price of the food and delivery, he'd add an extra meal if he could get Jonas as a recurring customer. It would be well worth it to the restaurant and to Jonas. Jonas thank the chef and they ended that call. Jonas checked his phone again. "A few more minutes." He didn't want to look too eager.

Smiling, he thought about seeing Brooke in the nude, Jonas shook his head as a wide smiled crossed his face. He liked that adventurous nature of Brooke. Young women were always adventurous. He'd forgotten that since he'd turned thirty five.

Brooke had suddenly become his kind of woman—beautiful, young, and not afraid to take chances. She may not have been his type in the beginning, but he would spend the time finding out if he'd been wrong about her, and try to fashion her into *his type.*

Jonas's pure woman had been Alexander Blackstone a perfect Dom to his brother, a loyal friend and confidant to him. Always up for a challenge, never wavering when he needed her, but she was his brother's wife, and he'd wished he could have met someone like Alex because he would have been stable by now. Not floundering and always in trouble, looking for that perfect woman who could have calmed him.

Alex would have provided the anchor he'd needed to navigate this crappy lonely life he'd found himself in.

Jonas thought that maybe Brooke would be the one to save him from himself. Since she was young, sexy and adventurous. Maybe he could make her into what Alex had been to Max. Maybe Brooke would become his Alex, his Dom and he'd never have to look at another woman for his desires again.

The way Max found everything in one woman, Jonas had hoped for that too. Youth, beauty, and sex. Sex with the right woman who knew how to push all his bottoms was the key to Jonas. He needed sex. All kinds of kinky sex. That's what Jonas hoped for dreamed and fantasized about.

One woman to satisfy his every desires.

Was he looking for a woman like Alex? The answer was *hell yes*. Jonas always wanted a woman like his brother, Maximillian, and now he thought he'd found her.

When he closed his gate and strolled down the path to the beach, he met Brooke strutting and facing him. Jonas stood smiling in the moonlight. He stood under a large florescent lamp that dotted along sections of the beach. Then he stepped away from the light to meet Brooke as she ran with a blanket draped over her shoulders, and into his arms.

He could only guess what was under the blanket, it made his heart race, and his balls tingle. She smiled when she opened the blanket under the brilliant moon shining down on the ocean and the two of them. Brooke stood looking at Jonas with a sexy closed grin showing off an amazing tanned body. She stepped back. Large breasts, pink nipples, and a small waist. Her thighs were toned. That much he knew from the beginning when he felt her hips and legs against his. But that wasn't what caught his attention. It had been her hairless mound.

Jonas ran his tongue over his top and bottom lip, salivated, then swallowed.

Jonas's erection grew painfully hard as he stood focused on Brooke's amazing young body. He reached for Brooke, and brought her into his arms, then he whispered breathlessly in her ear. "Fuck me but you're an amazing beautiful woman. He couldn't keep his cock from twitching, as it thumped against her soft skin.

"You look pretty amazing yourself," she replied looking up into his eyes when she placed her palms under Jonas's shirt and rubbing her hands up and down his chest. Jonas reached and brought the tee over his head then tossing it to the ground. "What gym do you work out in?" She questioned as she rubbed and palmed his hard muscular arms.

"We can talk about that later. We came here to swim, not talk about how I got these muscles or my tattoos."

"I like a man with tattoos," Brooke said, dipping her head to kiss the one on his chest. He wanted to stay on the beach and fuck her but Jonas thought that he should be a gentleman. He didn't want to scare her off. Not when he thought he'd found the right woman for him.

Jonas winked at her and stepped out of his shorts, kicked off his flip-flops, snatched the blanket from Brooke's shoulders threw it to the ground, and turned and ran into the surf.

"Fuck. It's cold. I didn't know it would be this cold." He shivered and Brooke pushed him down into the waves. "I thought Miami would be hot," he said taking her down with him as she laughed when she fell on top of him.

"Miami is hot, but the water is cool. Now you're not going to pussy out on me are you?"

Jonas glanced at Brooke, rolled her over on the sand, as the waves moved over them. He'd been called a lot of things but never a pussy.

Looking into her brown eyes he took her mouth hard. His tongue dipping inside her soft fleshy mouth. Then he pulled back.

"I'm not a pussy. I eat pussy for breakfast, dinner, and supper. I'm planning on having pussy for supper." He glanced down at Brooke and placed his hand between her legs feeling her clit ready to finger fuck her, but decided against it. *Everything in due time*, he thought. He needed to take his time with Brooke even though his cock didn't feel the same way. His dick had been ready to explode.

Then he pushed her into the water before he stood and reached for her wrist, hauling her up to face him. "Let's swim and then we eat," he chuckled.

· · · ·

THEY SWAM UNTIL BROOKE had gotten tired and started back to the lights, and Jonas swam behind her. When they reached the shore, Jonas helped her out and said, "I'm hungry. What about supper. You can have whatever you want. I ordered something for you from the local seafood restaurant. If you don't like it, they promised that they will get it to me fast. We can shower and you can have a drink.

You can eat whatever you want and after that, I plan on making my meal between your legs." He whispered as he took her hands and walked to where he dropped his clothes and the blanket.

"I think I've been out too long. I have to get back."

"What do you mean? You're not going to leave me like this?" Jonas questioned, holding his cock and stroking it. What about my supper? You gave me the impression that you wanted me, but I see you're nothing but a tease."

After Brooke covered her body and Jonas put on his pants, she strutted up to Jonas, both were wet. He opened the blanket and eased close to her. The blanket covered and absorbed some of the salty ocean water from their bodies, but added to the heat which burned inside Jonas.

Brooke eased close to Jonas. She leaned and placed a soft kiss on his lips. "I'm not a tease Jonas. I meant everything I said. I didn't know when I made this date with you that my boyfriend would call and tell me he'd be stopping over tonight. I wanted to be with you but—"

"Tell him to go fuck off," Jonas barked. Jonas had always been all or nothing. He would fall hard and fast for a woman, or he'd be cold and could never warm up to the wrong woman, but this time he'd fallen for Brooke and she was the right woman for him he told himself.

No one had to tell him, he felt it, he knew it, and he'd fallen fast and completely for Brooke. His mind and body had been a measurement. His mind knew, and his body knew better.

"I wish I could tell him to fuck off, but I can't do that because he pays for everything. You don't understand." Brooke placed her palm on his day old beard and passed it over the side of his face. Jonas leaned into her hand with closed eyes.

He opened his eyes and glared at her. "I can do that for you. Pay for everything you need. Tell him you want to be with me." Brooke stood back, and narrowed her eyes in disbelief.

"But I don't know you, Jonas, and you don't know me. We just met. There are things you don't know about me. I wish I could tell you and make you understand. If you knew the real me, you wouldn't want me."

This sounded to Jonas like a speech he'd given years before to his ex-wife when she wanted to know why he wouldn't commit to her.

"I know that I like you a lot and want to take care of you. What is there to know? You're a woman, and I'm a man who wants to be with you. And I can afford you. Is this man single?" Brooke took her time before she answered.

"He's married."

"Then why can't you tell him that you've found a single man and you want to be with him. I'm not married. I don't have anyone waiting for me to come home to them."

Brooked pulled away from Jonas. "I have to go. If you still want to see me, I'll come to your house tomorrow night. I don't have classes tomorrow, and I never see my boyfriend more than one day a week if that. This is the first time he's asked to see me twice in a week." Brooke lowered her head and started down a path that would lead her to her house, but she didn't get far before Jonas reached for her arm and she turned to lock eyes with him.

"Wait. You're in college?" Jonas questioned in disbelief.

"Yeah. I'm in college, and my boyfriend pays for that too." Brooked pulled away from Jonas's arms and walked away down a darkened path.

"I can pay for your college. Just you wait. I can do all the things that man is doing for you and more," Jonas shouted. His mouth turned downward in a sad expression. Brooked stopped and turned on the balls of her feet.

"It's not what he does for me, Jonas, but what he does to me and I do to him." Jonas didn't understand what she'd said or maybe he didn't want to understand. He knew that he liked everything about Brooke and he wanted to see her again. He wanted to caress her silky black hair, kiss her full lips, and taste her pussy.

He envied that man who could get close enough to Brooke to touch her the way he wanted to. He envied that man because he could be inside her body when he could not.

Closing the door behind him, he tramped over to the shower and stood in there for a long time. He needed to get off, he needed an orgasm, *but not with his hand again for fuck's sake*, he thought.

After Jonas's shower, he needed someone to talk to. He'd promised Alex that he'd call her, and yet he'd been too occupied with Brooke. Looking at the time in Miami, ten o'clock. "It's still early in Montana. It's eight," Jonas murmured.

Alex would be in her tub with the candles or if Max was home, she'd be in his room after they'd put the children to bed. "I want that kind of stable life," Jonas whispered into the empty room. Jonas reached for his phone.

"Alex. This is Jonas."

"I've been waiting for you to call. Are you alright?"

"You can say that. I just miss everyone. The children especially."

"You don't sound well. What's the problem besides being lonesome?" He heard the music in the background and he knew where Alex was. She had this wonderful old fashion looking tub in her bathroom.

It was her sanctuary and no one was allowed in there. Jonas had sneaked in there one day when she wasn't home. He wanted to buy perfume for his ex. He could have asked Alex but he didn't want her to know that the perfume she wore had been intoxicating. He'd lived for that smell on her whenever he got close to her.

"I'm doing fine."

"Are you taking your meds?" He wished she didn't ask that as if he was a child that forgot to brush his teeth. He never could get used to Alex treating him like a child. Maybe it was because of all the shit he'd gotten into and either she or Max had to intervene most of the time.

"Yeah. Yeah, Alex. I'm taking them. I didn't call you for you to question me on that. I have wonderful news. I've met someone."

"So soon? But then you're a handsome man. Any woman would find you attractive. You're such a good man, but don't you think it's too soon after your divorce from Crystal."

"Did you say that to Crystal when she couldn't wait to find someone and she was still married to me?" Jonas voice sounded harsh to Alex and she sat up in silence. "I'm sorry, Alex. You and I know that I'd been a fuck up before I met Crystal, and we should never have gotten married in the first place."

"Let's not talk about Crystal. You said you met someone. What's her name?"

"Her name is Brooke. That's all I know. We've just been skinning dipping and I think she's the one. I can feel it. I've never been as sure of anything in my life as this."

"Does she feel the same way about you? But of course she does. You're the second sexiest man alive. You know Max is the first," Alex said with a chuckle.

Nothing phased Jonas any more. Now being compared to Max because he'd finally found his soul mate, and no one and nothing would separate him from her. He made up his mind to do whatever it took to make her his.

Jonas must have fallen asleep after he hung up with Alex, nevertheless, Alex's reassurances about Brooke didn't keep him sleeping soundly, especially since he hadn't had a woman in months. All he had lately was his fist and that had grown old quickly. Not even his dick responded. The only time he'd felt anything was when Brooke exposed her beautiful naked body to him in the moonlight, and he'd been eager to feel her insides without cold ocean water between them.

Before going to bed he took his meds. He thought he'd been dreaming and he was back in New York at the club, or in Afghanistan when he heard a loud snap of leather, then a moan, a groan, and finally a scream. It was then he leapt out of bed in his boxers and rushed outside. It was coming from the second floor of Brooke's home. It had to be because there weren't many homes in the area, and most of them were vacant until the height of summer.

From where Jonas stood he had a clear view of Brooke's bedroom and there was a dim light in it. The rest of the house was dark except for that shadowy room on the second floor. With hardly any illumination coming from anywhere, there was a bright light in what he thought was her bathroom, and the darkness outside where he stood, he could see clearly.

It was the same man alright, but this time, there was someone else in her room. Jonas studied the shadow of another man standing in the doorway. Jonas couldn't see if he had anything in his hands, but what he'd been sure about was the manacles in his hand had been a pair of handcuffs. He'd known those anywhere. At his club he'd used them, but only when a woman wanted him to.

But it appeared that Brooke had been hesitant about the use of those cuffs by her shouting and pulling away from him. Brooke had been arguing with her boyfriend and maybe it was because of another man. Jonas didn't know which.

When she raised her hands in protest, Jonas saw that she wore a pair of handcuffs, he didn't miss her flawless nude body, her red buttocks, and the black leather riding crop her boyfriend held in his hands. And he didn't miss in the light he'd been right the first time, the boyfriend had to be around forty years old. Twenty years or more her senior.

When her boyfriend pushed her to the bed, that's when Jonas almost bolted to her door, but he thought better of it and stopped.

He'd owned clubs where women who were into BDSM enjoyed this treatment. He didn't know Brooke well enough to know if she'd fought back because the punishment wasn't severe enough, or whether it was too much and she'd given a safe word and it wasn't honored. He just didn't know.

He wanted Brooke but he didn't know if she wanted him and that's what stopped him from tearing through the bushes, kicking down the door, and beating the shit out of those two men. Thank God he didn't drink anymore what with the stand your ground laws in Florida, he didn't know if they carried a gun. He didn't have one because Max had taken them from him, afraid he get in trouble again.

Before Jonas turned to go back to his place, he glanced again and this time he heard Brooke laughing. When he looked up he saw Brooke lying across his knees as he sat on the bench in front of the bed. It was then Jonas realized that she must have enjoyed this. He watched as Brooke's boyfriend gave her several smacks on her already blistered ass with his palms, then smoothed his hands over her red ass cheeks, smacked her hard with one hand, and threatened her with the crop. She never stopped laughing and groaning with pleasure.

The second man had come into the room, faced Brooke's buttocks, and with one hand dangling handcuffs and with the other, he'd stroked his cock before dropping the handcuffs on the bed, and placing a condom on his shaft.

Jonas watched as her boyfriend leaned over, kissed her ass, reached and opened her ass cheeks and the other man kneeled, then placed his face between her cheeks, licked, bit, and kissed her as the three of them moaned, and groaned with blissful pleasure.

When the other man stopped, Brooke rose from lying across his lap, stood in front of her boyfriend where he brought her to him still sitting, and he leaned and kissed her stomach. She leaned in, took a fist full of his hair and brought her mound to his face. He buried his face in her pubic area—licking and opening her folds to place his tongue inside her opening.

As the boyfriend licked her from the front, the man, fucked her from the back.

Finally Jonas got it. Brooke did say that Jonas didn't know anything about her. Now he knew enough. But then there may have been more to know. He saw a leather corset draped across a chair, over it laid a whip, and near the legs of the chair, a pair of high-heeled black leather boots.

Now the picture had been complete—she'd been the Dom to these men. She owned them, they did her bidding. Not the other way around.

One last look and Jonas realized that everyone had been naked. The only one not naked was Brooke's boyfriend. *The forty something freak,* Jonas thought.

Why would he bring in someone else to fuck Brooke? What were those two men going to do to her? Jonas didn't want to know the answer. Yet he did and he knew that his first thoughts were the correct ones and it didn't matter what he'd thought of her as being an innocent player in this game, she wasn't. The only thing she'd been innocent of was being very young and someone had to have molded her into the Dom she'd become.

Why did he ask that question, when he knew the answer? And that answer would make him sick to his stomach and weak because he needed and wanted Brooke but he'd wanted to mold her into his Dom.

He'd seen all kinds of men pass through his clubs in San Francisco and New York. Some who wanted to be whipped and some who enjoyed flogging and fucking women. He'd seen the ones who got off watching other men fuck a woman and on and on. Nothing surprised Jonas. Not even the art of sexual asphyxiation with ties or ropes.

The sexual asphyxiation had gotten him in trouble in New York. He didn't pay attention to his clientele and what was going on inside his club. Therefore, when he discovered a woman dead, he knew he'd been fucked and that's how he'd gotten Alex involved. And that's why he and his twin brother Max became estranged. He'd asked Alex to help him out of that serious fucking problem and to his surprise—she did.

He had a few regrets, maybe not a few but many, but opening his club wasn't one of them. Operating his BDSM clubs had been therapy for him. He'd been damaged by his time in the service and the only thing that could ease his pain was to learn the art of bondage. That's how he'd met Alex. His brother Max met her first. Max been a constant visitor of one of Jonas's clubs because not one brother had a secret, but both brothers had problems, but chose the same routes to solve them in different ways.

Jonas understood that there were all kinds of kinks that men and women engaged in. Some men enjoyed kissing women's feet, and some women catered to those kind of men. But he didn't know what kind of kink Brooke enjoyed, except the obvious ones. Did she like to display men and make them submit in front of others? Did she enjoy fucking men with a dildo or did she like being whipped and then turn on the men and abuse them. The possibilities had been endless and Jonas knew it from his dealing with all kinds of men and women in his BDSM clubs.

He didn't know Brooke. It could be more complicated than what he'd seen so far. He didn't know the full extent of her involvement with BDSM.

Rationalizing that everyone had some form of sexual deviancy was the only way Jonas could accept the idea that he wanted Brooke whatever way he could get her. After all they weren't too different. He and Brooke may have been more alike than any women he'd met so far. Some individuals chose to act on their sexual urges and desires and some chose to bury them. He understood her and that led him to believe that there was no reason to rule out a relationship with Brooke.

He wanted Brooke to himself and if they were going to have a Dom/sub relationship, it would have to be one where only he and she served each other's needs, because he was like his brother Max in that way. He didn't like to share.

# Chapter 8

Jonas made an appointment to see the realtor who handled the selling of the strip mall. He could have made arrangements online, however, when he called, a voice of an older woman answered the phone.

"Hi, my name is Jonas and I'd like to make an appointment to see a certain property your client has for sale." She didn't ask what property and Jonas assumed that she had only one at the time.

"Yes, Jonas, and how did you hear about the property?"

"I spotted it as I drove by and I just love the location. I'm new in town."

"You know you could see everything online and—" Jonas didn't let her complete the statement.

"I know, but seeing it in person is not like walking in each room, getting the feel and smell of the place."

"You're very perceptive, Jonas. Business is done on line now, and some of the younger realtors have no feel for that special touch. They don't want to meet their clients, they want the clients to do all the work, and then they come in and reap the rewards. I, however, will meet you at your own convenience and show you the property. What time would be great for you, Jonas?"

"It's Jonas Blackstone, give me an hour, and I'll meet you there if that's okay with you."

"That's fine. You're such a polite man. I'm sure you'll like what you see."

. . . .

THE STORES WERE LOCATED in a developed busy area right off the beach, the place was small, but Jonas knew it's potential, even though the area had only a few shops. He thought it was just enough space for him to handle alone. Maybe he'd hire a personal assistant to take care of the social media stuff. He'd never been an extrovert, otherwise he'd been a politician. Max had been his opposite. More sociable than him even before going into the Marines.

He'd have to hire someone to advertise for him if he wanted his business to fulfill its potential and make the money he'd need to thrive on his own. Jonas didn't like the time it took to post on a blog, getting a website up for his business, tweeting, Facebook, and all the media at his disposal that he had to be a part of to get the word out.

If he didn't hire someone for that shit, he'd probably say something that would have the FBI at his door, and with all that had happened to him, he was lucky he hadn't been arrested by now. He'd been happy to keep a low profile, and remain in the shadows.

Jonas hadn't even thought about a name for the bar yet. What the fuck could he call it? All the good names were taken. As he drove to the location, he thought about what he could name it and said the name out loud to hear how it sounded.

"What about Crazy Cock? No. No. Then everyone will think it's a gay bar and only a few will come. I want everyone straight and gay, old and young to drink and enjoy themselves," Jonas murmured as he drove into the parking space in front of the strip mall where there sat a late model white Lexus.

Yes he'd been right. A bar in this location appeared perfect. Sitting and looking around, Jonas believed this place, with this location, would bring in the most money for him. Yes bars usually did where there were young men and women partying all times of the year. There was the matter of getting a liquor license, which he didn't think would be a problem.

As a veteran he could get certain types of vendor licenses, and because of that, he felt sure that no one would stop him from trying to make a living even if he was a rich, but they didn't know that. However, the minute they heard the Blackstone name they would put things together.

*Did Max have to plaster the Blackstone name on just about every building from the Pacific Ocean to the Atlantic Ocean and the Gulf of Mexico?*

"A man has to work, regardless if he has money." That's what Max had preached to Jonas after finding him on the street homeless, and placing him in the hospital to get him mental and physical care.

Jonas smiled because he felt for once he'd done the right thing. The stores would bring in a nice income to pay for this investment. The extra income from the other shops, along with the bar would give him a faster return on his money.

A bar in that area near the beach was an ideal place, and a business he knew he could handle without putting out lots of money as he'd done in New York, where he'd sunk a fortune into the Bondage Club only to lose that fortune. He knew he'd fucked up half the money left him by his parents, and at the rate he was going, he'd be broke by forty. Therefore, he had to make this work because he didn't want Max to say that he'd fucked up again. The disappointed look on Max's face had been more painful than losing the money.

Jonas's thoughts had wandered like they often did, but now he focused on the place in front of him. If he purchased and refurbished the building, he could rent to high end shops, and a restaurant. At least those were his plans. With an upscale restaurant, he'd get people with money and willing to spend it. "This is perfect," Jonas heard himself say out loud.

Looking to his right, there were condo's everywhere, no shops, local restaurants, or bars where young men and woman could hangout, or the older crowd where they could take a walk and have a drink, and then leave the night life to the younger men and women. If he managed to swing this, get the right price, he'd have business day and night.

If he installed the right fixtures in the bar, and made it conducive for the younger crowd, it would pay for itself over night. Jonas smiled. For the first time he would do something on his own and not need Max to contribute, or bail him out of another mess.

Jonas had been determined not to fuck this up this time. He stepped out of his corvette and entered the unlocked door. Looking around Dottie came into view as she met him coming through the door. She smiled at him and extended her hand.

"Mr. Blackstone. Are you *the* Mr. Blackstone?" Dottie asked with a wide smile. A middle age woman with blond hair and blue eyes who had seen too much sun, and more than enough life, questioned. She wore a conservative cheap pink suit which did nothing for her figure, but she wore a beautiful smile, had lovely pulled skin which made her look ten years younger than fifty, which Jonas thought she was.

"Not only are you good-looking and handsome, you're sexy too. You don't get that much package in one man these days in Miami. You may get that in gay men, but you're straight as they come, aren't you?" Dottie's face lit up thinking about the possibilities, and had she been twenty years younger.

"Does it matter?"

"Of course not, Mr. Blackstone."

"But for your ears only, I'm straight," Jonas whispered. Her smile beamed as she held on to Jonas's hand and walked around showing him the place.

Jonas chuckled, letting her have a moment. He looked at her because he knew where she'd spent her money—on a plastic surgeon and a dentist. Jonas smiled at her and she returned the gesture. Then he recovered his hand, walked around touching, looking at the place, making a mental picture of where he wanted the bar installed.

Turning to face Dottie he admitted, "I'm Max's brother if you're speaking of Maximillian Blackstone—" Dottie's smile widen as she cut Jonas off before he had a chance to complete his statement.

"That's exactly who I'm talking about. Are you buying this for Maximillian Blackstone?"

"No. It's for me." The realtor turned and faced Jonas and offered him a wider smile.

"There's no problem either way. If your brother is in the market for a home or property in Miami, I hope you give him my card. And that goes for you too." Dottie reached into her purse hanging on her shoulder, and flicked the card into Jonas's hand.

When Jonas placed the card in his pocket, Dottie stood in his way and said, "The name Blackstone will get you anything you need in this town." *Will it get me the woman I want?* That's the question that crossed Jonas's mind. "Just tell me if you want the place, or take your time and decide. Between you and me, I haven't had many queries about it lately. It's just setting there. I know the owner would like for someone to take it off his hands. I think I can get you a good deal." Dottie offered.

"It would be good for me if I can sell it and I know by the look on your face you want this particular property."

"You're right, I do want the property."

"I assume you have a lawyer?" Dottie questioned, "To look over the papers once you decide."

Jonas focused on what Dottie had said and not the club. "Yes, of course I have a lawyer." He didn't have one, but he knew how to find one in a hurry. On the internet. But he didn't tell her that. He was in too much of a hurry to get back home, because tonight was the night he'd have a talk with Brooke and hopefully they'd do much more than talk.

After settling up with Dottie, Jonas drove home.

# Chapter 9

Pulling into the driveway, Jonas sat for a few minutes looking around. He'd placed his hand over his chin and chuckled. He liked this place Miami. He could make his fortune and become respectable, he thought, especially since he believed everyone were as pleasant, laidback and accommodating as Dottie. So far he hadn't been wrong. It wasn't like New York where everywhere he'd turned people were out to get something from him. Here in Miami they were here to have fun and enjoy life.

Jonas parked the Corvette in front of his rented house, hopped out, and rushed inside to pick up clothes and packages he hadn't bother with. He'd bought clothes for his life in Miami, and the packages had been scattered around the large home because he didn't think about placing them in the trash. What day would that be? He didn't know anything about living alone and especially in a home. He'd always had someone he'd paid to take care of that.

Now with funds low because he'd fucked up lots of money on his Bondage Club in New York, he'd have to rely on what Max had placed into his account.

Picking up his clothes he realized that he'd made such a mess. He didn't have people cleaning and cooking for him and he'd have to arrange that especially since he'd need time to get the bar up and running.

After clearing the house of clothes and throwing them into the closet, Jonas still had the seafood from last night in the fridge, but he didn't know how long sushi lasted and he didn't want to take any chances, so he emptied it into the trash. "Pizza and a beer that's good," he murmured as he raced around the kitchen to place some of the unwashed plates and glasses into the dishwasher, and get rid of the old coffee in the coffee maker.

Then he hurried to the shower, took a quick one and was out when the bell rang. Reaching for his robe, he shrugged his arms through and opened the door. The pizza was on time. But where was Brooke?

When Jonas paid the pizza guy and brought it to the kitchen, and on his way to his bedroom, another ring. He sauntered to the door barefoot, still wearing his robe, and opened the door without checking because he thought the delivery guy had forgotten to give him his free drink.

Relief washed over him, and there stood this gorgeous beauty dressed in a pair of white slacks and white linen blouse and high-heeled sandals.

Jonas couldn't believe his eyes. Her long flowing dark hair, flawless skin with plump lips covered with pink lipstick had him mesmerize that he'd almost forgot how she looked last night. "You're beautiful," Jonas whispered as his eyes brightened and his cock stirred beneath the robe.

"Can I come in? I don't want to stand out here," Brooke said slanting her head to the side wearing a closed smile.

"Oh sure, of course," Jonas said his hand trembling as he took hers.

"I've never met anyone as pretty as you. I mean I have, but I've never had a woman that I've liked in my presence as beautiful as you," Jonas confessed nervous, walked beside Brooke leading her into the living area. Brooke sauntered ahead of Jonas as his eyes captured her curvy body. She appeared taller because of her high heels, before she'd come to him on the beach barefoot.

Brooke sat down as Jonas stood looking at her. Then he caught himself. "Would you like a beer?"

"I'd prefer something stronger if you have it." Jonas fumbled around a cabinet where he thought the liquor might be. He'd stopped drinking since he'd come from New York and been sober for a year or more. He'd promised Max and Alex that he'd clean out and so he did. There had been more to think about than himself. His child with

Crystal and Max's children. Jonas wanted to be a good example, and yet Max had told him to leave.

He'd only had one drink that night before he left for Florida, and he realized that he didn't have a taste for it anymore. But tonight he'd given himself permission to have a beer since he didn't black out whenever he'd drank beers.

Jonas found a bottle of vodka probably from the last renters who'd leased the house. Jonas rented it furnished at the last minute on his long ride to Florida. He'd wired the money and the house was his for however long he needed it.

"Is vodka okay?" Jonas inquired, turning with the bottle in his hand.

"That's my drink. I'll have a shot." Searching around, Jonas found shot glasses and poured Brooke one.

"I'm only having beer." He handed Brooke the shot glass with vodka.

Brooke titled her chin up and drank it fast. When she'd downed that, she asked for another. Jonas didn't want to lecture her because he detested lectures, but he thought she was too pretty and too young for him not to say something, and he more than liked that young beautiful girl. "You should have something to eat first. I have a pizza and it's still hot." Jonas hurried to the counter island, and opened the box to show her.

Brooke agreed. Jonas had soft music playing in the background as she sat down at the bar. He wanted mood music not dancing music because he didn't want to dance, he wanted to make love to Brooke in a serious way. He'd wanted to get close to her and now he had his chance.

Picking up a piece of pizza, Brooke glanced over at Jonas. "What's a tall handsome man doing alone?"

"I'm not alone. I'm with you." She smiled and ate the pizza.

"I don't mean that," she said locking eyes with him. "You're so good-looking I can't believe that you have no one."

Jonas walked up behind Brooke, leaned and kissed her on her neck. His warm mouth inched up and finally made its way to her ear where he whispered, "I'm hoping to make you mine and soon. I have plans for you Brooke, and as soon as I learn your last name I'm going to ask you to marry me."

"You know nothing about me."

"When you tell me your surname, then I'll know everything I need to know about you because soon everyone will call you Mrs. Blackstone. There's only one other woman that has that distinction, and she's married to my brother Max. See you know I have a brother, and you still haven't told me about yourself."

"It's Cartwright. Brooke Cartwright. Now let's not talk about me or you. I need to eat, so I can get back to drinking. The world appears pleasant when I'm drunk." Jonas remembered when he thought like that. He'd lost his parents, and joined the Marines. It was the drinking that appeared to make his life less stressful, and he was about Brooke's age then.

After they ate and Brooke had too many shots, she started unbuttoning her clothing and since Jonas hadn't had time to dress before Brooke arrived at his front door, it was perfect for him.

"Will you take off my shoes?" she questioned watching Jonas intently. *Oh she loves to have control over a man,* he thought peering at her. Jonas had misdiagnosed her initially. She wanted to control Jonas. He'd been with women who loved to punish men and a good many deserved to be flogged. And he was among them.

Jonas hadn't hung around looking long enough to see the entirety of what went on in that bedroom last night. That's why he hadn't come to the right conclusions about Brooke. But he was coming to the right conclusions now. He'd known women almost like Brooke, but they were much older than she. Someone must have taught her. Maybe a man, he thought, or she'd had been in too many immoral situations in her short life. He didn't want to guess which ones. They both had hard times, and now he wanted to change that.

Jonas wanted to be with Brooke. Take her away from men who would use her and give her a different life. He had started over many times, and now he wanted that for the girl he'd found himself falling in love with.

It was Brooke who had all the control, and it was her who allowed her boyfriend to spank her. They probably played games that way he thought. It wasn't the first time he'd seen this, but not with a woman as young as Brooke. It takes years to learn to control men and become a master at Bondage and S&M, but from the little Jonas had seen Brooke was a Master.

Jonas admitted to himself that he didn't want that any more. He wanted a woman for his own, and if he would play games, it would just be the two of them. He wanted a relationship like the kind his brother Max and Alex had, and he wanted a family of his own with that type of woman who wouldn't want to control him completely where'd she'd chain him, order him around, and bring him to clubs to demonstrate how dominant she'd been in their relationship.

Jonas had been determined to find out if Brooke was who he needed in his life now that he was starting over again.

When Brooke stripped off her clothes, stood in front of Jonas as he'd discarded the last of her shoes, and Jonas was still on his knees with his robe on when she moved her hips close to his face, reached for his thick dark curls, took a fist of his hair, and pulled it up where his eyes were locked into hers. "You have wonderful blue eyes. A bit sad. But I can make you happy, Jonas."

Brooke didn't need to sell herself to him. Jonas had been blown away with her since the day he laid eyes on her.

"Do you want me?" She whispered in a quiet voice looking down on Jonas. Hell yeah Jonas wanted her. His cock was throbbing and pre-cum had rubbed against the fabric of his white robe. All he could do was nod as she braced her hips to his face and pulled his hair forward as she opened her legs wide.

With his mouth on her mound, his tongue on her clit, between her folds, and his face taking in her natural scent, where he smelled the strawberry body wash, he grabbed her ass cheeks with his large hands and brought her body close to his face, rubbing his face in her shaved mound.

Jonas used his tongue to tease her trembling clit, and when Jonas's warm tongue touched it lightly, his mouth covered her folds, and he began sucking her clit hard.

Breathlessly she moaned and punched her hips forward as she groaned in pleasure and with each suck she tightened her fist around Jonas's curls. Half panting and breathing hard Brooke said, "I told my boyfriend that it was off. I told him to go fuck off. I want to be with you, Jonas," she groaned out in pleasure. "Did you mean what you said?"

Jonas leaned back panting, one fist on his hard length, stroking it from the base to the tip looking up at Brooke, "Fuck yeah. I want to take care of you. I want you to be mine. All mine. I don't want you to belong to anyone but me."

"I'm yours now. And you're mine." And Jonas rested his face between Brooke's hard thighs, and she dry fucked his face as he sucked her clit. Then she let out a loud moan. "I want you to fuck me hard, Jonas. As hard as you can."

Jonas leaned back and reached for her arm and pulled Brooke to the floor, and with his hard cock in his hand, he entered Brooke fast and hard. He'd forgotten about his condom. He forgot everything and everybody except how wonderful her body felt underneath his, and how tight her pussy felt at that moment.

"Oh God this is good," Jonas groaned wishing he'd never stop fucking Brooke. Wishing he could go on all night and all day.

His hard body on top of her felt like heaven when he'd pushed his length in and pulled out of her warm wet flesh. He leaned over her looking into her bright brown eyes filled with lust. He lowered his mouth over hers, and she offered him her tongue as it split through his lips. Jonas had been ready to cum from the first time he saw her and when he peered at her when he heard her scream. He had his hand on his cock fighting back an orgasm when he saw her naked and her boyfriend whipping her pretty ass.

Now his orgasm rushed through his body down to his groin through his cock's head, into Brooke's warm insides, when his mouth crushed hers, and their tongues mingled and she bit his shoulder and screamed.

His body tightened and his swollen cock's head expanded inside her warm tight body releasing ropes of cum. Jonas nipped and kissed her neck, pinched her nipples hard, as Brooke scratched, bit, and sucked on the shoulder. "Take me from behind," she insisted. *My kind of woman*, he thought.

"Are you sure? I have to get a condom."

"Of course I'm sure. I have some over there with my pants." Jonas reached for her pants, pulled the condom out of her pocket, placed the packet in his mouth, tore it removing the condom, and sliding it over his still hard as a rock length.

Jonas watched as Brook got on all fours when he sat back on his knees adjusting the condom. He reached for her round hips and brought her to him. She craned her head to the side, "Slap my ass hard. I want to feel it, and then drive inside of me."

"Without lubricant?" Jonas questioned.

"There's enough on the condom. Don't worry, you won't hurt me. Once you have it all inside my ring, the pain will go away. That's when we will both enjoy each other," she assured Jonas.

Jonas knew, but he'd never tell her how he knew about anal intercourse, at least until they became better acquainted with each other, and then they would have more time to express their sexual likes and dislikes. Jonas learned that those were important things which made sex more enjoyable. Jonas knew little about Brooke, but he knew that she enjoyed him eating her, and she liked rough sex.

He slapped her hard on her ass.

"Harder, Jonas." Jonas did it again still not using all his strength. "I need to feel it." Her ass-cheeks were red on that last hit. He heard her breathing, he felt her taut nipples, and they were stiff. "Now put it in fast." Jonas reached for his length and drove it all into her, and she never winced or let out a cry. She groaned and pushed her butt into Jonas causing his cock to go in deeper.

Holding on to her hips he pushed in, drove deep inside her fast and furious as his breathing became shallow and quick. He glanced down at her perfect full ass, his heart raced, and he pounded deeper inside Brooke. When he looked down on her flawless skin, with his hard cock lodged inside her, he thought how beautiful, sexy and hot and what an arousing sight with her on all fours with him behind her tunneling into her ass.

"Pull your dick out and take off the condom and fuck me. I want to feel you," Brooke commanded. Jonas could hardly catch his breath before she wanted something else and he was willing to give her whatever she needed to satisfy her sexually. He stayed hard. Maybe it was the drugs the doctors prescribed, maybe it was Brooke being so sexy, or maybe it was just that for the first time he found someone that turned him on and he was sober. He didn't know what it was and he didn't care. He thought this was it. He'd found a woman for him.

Jonas wished he known Brooke before he'd gotten involved with the last woman he'd had sex with. She enjoyed being whipped before sex. He didn't mind that, but she wanted to be choked as he fucked her. If he'd known that about her, he'd never gotten involved with her.

He enjoyed rough sex as much as the next man, but he had to tell her to go. He wished he hadn't because it was then she'd been found dead in his club, and he been forced to get Alex involved.

But he didn't want to think about that now, especially since he had this beautiful young woman who had just said she told her boyfriend that she wanted to be with him, and for him to go fuck himself. That had turned Jonas on more than Brooke telling him to fuck her in the ass. Brooke like to be fucked in her ass, and Jonas was always up for the challenge.

As long as that wasn't all she wanted.

The secrets that may have existed between the two of them were slowly becoming no secrets at all. They appeared to like each other and fell effortlessly into each other's sexual desires.

Jonas placed one hand over her ass and another on her stomach to anchor her. His hand

moved down to her pussy. He felt her clit quiver on his finger, and on the final push into her opening, he emptied his salty clear cum inside her tight ring of muscles. Brooke tightened her insides around his swollen cock, forcing more cum out of him. Then her body trembled and shook when she screamed, "I'm coming, Jonas, eat me."

Jonas pulled out, flipped Brooke on her back, opened her legs, and he was face deep into her mound licking and sucking as she wrapped her legs around his neck with his tongue deep inside her bringing her to orgasm.

# Chapter 10

When Jonas turned and looked at Brooke, the sun had spilled through the shutters and into the room. He shook his head and smiled couldn't believe his luck. He gazed at her, his desire and affection for her—boundless. He couldn't imagined that he'd been this fortunate to find a woman made just for him. Who knew that a feeling of complete happiness would ever come to him? Not Jonas of course. He'd known that Max would have happiness with a wife he'd adored, a family life with children, but he didn't dare dream that this could come to him.

Now he envisioned his life taking a different and complete turn for the best.

Jonas saw himself waking up in the morning married, and this time happy with his choice of female. He imagined great sex with a beautiful desirable young woman. Yes, he was maybe ten years her senior, but who the fucked cared if they didn't.

Their differences and likes would make the journey of life more exciting. He could show her places, and give her things she'd could only dream about. Buy her a home, give her a palace if she asked him.

Whatever the fuck her young heart desired he'd make that come true.

Jonas reached for Brooke and brought her into his arms. Somehow she'd rolled over away from him on the other side of the Californian King bed. That's when he'd felt the loss of her warm body. He hadn't slept with a woman in years.

He couldn't remember the last one. Maybe Crystal, but he couldn't remember when that was because each time they'd gotten together he'd have to leave. It was one thing or the other—someone found dead at one of his clubs, a woman who fell in love with him, because he'd tied her up and fucked her, because her husband—wouldn't handcuff her, or fuck her so he did, and she'd threatened to kill herself or him. Always something because of the choices he'd made.

He'd wondered how long Crystal would put up with him telling her that he had to work. Obviously not long. He didn't have to wait as long as he thought. When he did return to Crystal and their child, she'd had another child, and she'd moved on. He didn't ask for a blood test to prove that the child was his. He didn't remember much and assumed it was his and paid for everything. Crystal had gotten her divorce while he was in New York, when he couldn't be bothered to open the court papers, because he'd gotten himself embroiled in yet another murder.

"It's the business you're in," Max warned. "Get out before you lose your mind, or go to jail. You can't survive in jail. Not because you're weak, Jonas, but because you never could handle being cooped up anywhere."

At the time Jonas thought when he'd opened those Bondage clubs they weren't work. It was therapy. At first, the clubs were far cheaper than spending thousands of dollars to get someone to listen to him bare his soul. Jonas thought the clubs were a way to channel his energy and relieve some of the pain and memories of war.

Jonas looked for every excuse not to go back to Seattle to be with Crystal and their baby. In truth it wasn't her he wanted to be with. The woman he'd wanted was the one married to his brother, and now he had one, he thought, could measure up to Alex. He could wipe Alex out of his mind, and be done with his obsession.

Pulling Brooke into his arms she opened her eyes and flashed a beautiful warm smile his way. Taking his hand, he removed a large swath of hair from her face. "Do you know how beautiful you are lying in my arms?" Jonas lowered his head and kissed her lightly on her plump pink lips.

"Do you know how handsome you are, Mr. Blackstone?" Jonas pulled her closer and held her tighter. Then he kissed her on her forehead, making his way down to her lips once more where he brushed over them lightly hoping for much more. Brooke turned her head.

"You don't want to kiss me?" Jonas questioned.

"I need to brush my teeth first."

Jonas placed his finger between her legs, found her opening, and inserted his finger. Brooked squirmed with an opened mouth, parted her lips and a pleasurable moan escaped her mouth. When Jonas pulled out his finger, he placed it to his nose. "I love your scent. Men are attracted to their mates because of scents."

"You mean animals are attracted to their mates because of scents." Jonas raised an eyebrow. "I'm in college and that's first year biology." Jonas wasn't sure. He didn't recall that from any of his biology classes. Well he never even took biology if he remembered correctly.

"In any case, I love the way you smell early in the morning, and I don't care about you brushing your teeth, or taking a shower before I fuck you. When I was in the Marines—"

"You were in the Marines?"

"Remind me to tell you about my time in Afghanistan. Only when we have lots of babies, and I'm too old to remember the stories correctly. In which case, I'll never tell you." Brooke and Jonas chuckled.

"Jonas Blackstone you make me happy. I don't know when I've laughed more and felt at peace." Jonas glanced over at Brooke. He'd felt the same way since arriving in Miami, and meeting Brooke.

"Where are you going?" Brooked questioned, as Jonas rose then stepping out of the bed on to the hardwood floor.

"You need something to eat and didn't you say you have classes tonight. If I read the sun correctly, we've been in bed half the day. It's late. It's probably two pm."

"You're not in the desert and there are clocks. And no it isn't two it's three and you're right. I have a six o'clock class.

"And you're going to need something to eat. I warn you the only thing I can do is place toast in the toaster, coffee in the coffee maker, and order out. Since we don't have time to order anything to eat now—"

"Toast and coffee is fine. I'm easy and I can get a burger at school if I get hungry."

. . . .

WHEN BROOKE DRESSED and headed for the kitchen she didn't expect a wonderful breakfast of bread an assortment of jams, and fruit. Reaching for the bread, before eating, she leaned over and kissed Jonas.

"I can see myself in the mornings taking care of you," Jonas confessed. He wanted to play the submissive after being the Dominant for far too long.

"And if you burn my breakfast, I'll make you sit at my feet with a collar while we eat."

"I'll hire a cook and a maid and you can go to college or whatever your heart desires and when you get home, I'll have your bath waiting." Jonas saw Brooke turn away from him and he reached with his fingers and brought her lovely face back to meet his and their eyes locked. Blue on brown. "Is something wrong Brooke?"

"Nothing. Sometimes I can see this happening, but I wonder if it ever will. I've had too many disappointments in my life. I can't believe you're real. Are you real, Jonas?"

Jonas walked around and sat at the kitchen island next to Brooke. "I'm real and the life we want together will come true. Just wait until I tell my brother Max and his wife Alex. You will have everything you've wanted in life."

"All I want is you, Jonas. No one but you. I knew what I wanted the moment I saw you."

"And so did I, baby," Jonas admitted. They sat and drank coffee and ate the brunch Jonas had prepared.

"I hope you don't mind, but I'd like to go home and then drive to school."

"I don't mind at all. We overslept and there are things I have to take care of that I didn't get a chance to do before. I'm buying a mall."

Brooke glanced up, "You have that kind of money."

"I do but my sister in law is going to help me out. I don't want to ask my brother who's over the estate. She agreed to make me a loan. I'm planning on opening a bar, and the place is near the beach. It's in walking distance, and the college crowd can come out of the surf, and fall into my bar. I don't have a name for it yet but soon. I need to finalize the papers with this realtor who is eager to make some money. However, first I have to contact a lawyer. Do you know any lawyers?"

"I'm sorry, Jonas. I wished I did. I don't have a need for lawyers. I don't have any money."

"How do you pay for that home and car?" Jonas asked.

"It doesn't belong to me. I have access to them as long as I'm with Mark."

"Who is Mark?"

"The man you saw me with the other night. I knew you were there. I just wanted to know if you knew everything about me, whether you would want me, or not. I got my answer. That's why I told Mark to go fuck himself. He wanted to bring other men in to fuck me because he can't. I tie him up and use a whip on his ass then he likes to watch men fuck me and—"

"I don't want to know about anything else in your life. You're going to start over with me. We're both starting over. Now go get your clothes, better yet don't take any clothes. Leave Mark a note and the keys to the house and car. I'll pay for everything and I don't want anything from you, but your word that you're mine, and you don't belong to anyone else. You can have your freedom to go and come as you wish. When you're tired of me then you can leave and I'll give you whatever you want to take care of you."

Brooke glanced over at Jonas and tears welled in her eyes. "I don't want to be with anyone else. You're all I want and all I've ever hoped for, Jonas." She wrapped her arms around Jonas's neck and he picked her up and carried her into the bed room.

When they emerged, Brooke had a half hour to get back to the house, drop the keys, get the car, and rush to school. She'd planned on calling Mark and telling him where he could find the keys in the car, and put that life with him to rest.

After kissing Jonas, Brooke left to head out to school and Jonas called Dottie to tell her he'd be late. But first he needed to call Alex. He wanted Alex to know how happy he was and that he'd found his Alex.

"Alex how are you?"

As usual it's snowing, it's a snow day, and the children are home but Max isn't. Enough of me. How are you? What's going on? Now that you've had a chance to look over Miami what do you think?"

"I'll tell you later when I've had a chance to enjoy the place. Right now I'm trying to buy this place that looks like a good investment. But that's another story, and the truth, I called you because I knew you'd be happy for me. I found a woman. Just like you."

There was a long silence. "Are you there, Alex?"

"I'm here."

"Why the silence? Don't you want me to be happy?"

"Of course. I wish you all the happiness in the world, but holding me up as a measurement for the type of woman you're looking for isn't fair to the woman, or me. I've had a lot of bad breaks in my life and good ones when I met Max. But you know all the drama that's involved with being a part of this family. I never thought—"

"You never thought that I'd find anyone for me. I know I'm a lot of things Alex, but I believed you were the main one who would want me to be with someone like me and like you."

"What does that mean?" Alex questioned.

"You know what it means. You can't hold on to both of us—"

"You are wrong, Jonas. There are a lot of things about you that I've been wrong about, but I know in my heart that I'm not wrong now.

You'll have to face it that I won't be that other half of Max you want." Another long silence. "Tell me about her," Alex said, with a sigh that was so loud that Jonas heard it, yet he didn't say anything. He wanted to tell Alex about Brooke. He'd been so full with love that he had to tell someone, or he'd die.

He told Alex her complete name, and that he'd only know her for a day at most, she was beautiful just like Alex, she had amber eyes, and he'd fallen in love with her at first sight.

Wasn't that the same when Alex knew she'd fallen in love with Max and had to find him and make him pay attention to her? Brooke had been about the same age when Alex met Max if Jonas remembered correctly.

"Does she love you, Jonas?"

"She said she did. That's good enough for me." Alex knew that Jonas loved easily and often, but she didn't want to spoil his happiness. If he thought Brooke loved him that was good enough for her, for now. Furthermore, she'd prayed that Jonas would find a woman that kept him out of trouble so she could go on with her family, and devote herself to Max and the children. That had been a dream of hers since she'd met Max. Just be a loving sexy woman for his eyes only and bring some stability into their home.

"Alex? Alex are you there?"

"Yes, Jonas."

"I'm going to ask her to marry me as soon as I get the bar up and running, and I want you and Max to be at the wedding. Can you promise me that you will be there?"

"Of course, Jonas. Just tell me the date and I'll tell Max. I can't get the kids out of school so don't expect them."

A moment of silence was all Alex heard and perhaps she felt she'd hurt Jonas. She never wanted to hurt him, she thought he was fragile and Alex thought she should say something. "I can't promise you that they'll come, but we'll see. I have to check with Max first."

"As long as you and Max are here. That's all I ask for." There was hope in Jonas's voice when he hit the red button. He held the phone close to his heart. It had been great hearing Alex's voice again and as often. He'd missed her so much. Just talking to her wouldn't do it for him. He had to see her one more time before he'd get married again, but this time it would be different.

# Chapter 11

Months passed, Brooke moved in with Jonas and he'd been so busy getting the bar together for its big opening that he'd forgotten that it had been over six months with the purchasing of the building, liquor license, arrangement for his wedding and reception at the bar on Saturday, and other shit he hadn't thought about.

Brooke had been busy with her semester finals and he'd rarely gotten a chance to talk to her at night. She'd come to the bar and helped by giving him ideas about how to decorate the bar, she'd studied until all hours of the night, fell asleep, and he'd have to carry her to the car and into the house.

When he arrived home early in the morning, the sun was rising and he placed Brooke in the bed. He knew she should have been home sooner, but she wanted to stay with him. Brooke never liked to be alone especially since she'd broken up with her boyfriend Mark. Jonas didn't know why she'd felt that way and he didn't ask her. He didn't have the time, but after they were married, he'd have more than enough time.

He'd hired a bar manager and all the personnel he needed and he was moving into a new home. Dottie had made a fortune on Jonas. He didn't mind because now he had a new best friend who could pull strings for him, and she knew all the best people in Miami. The ones who could get him what he needed for his business.

When Jonas stepped into his home, Alex stepped out of the cab at the front door of Jonas's rental. Alex rang the bell as Jonas laid Brooke on the mattress. "Where are you going, Jonas?" Brooke purred. "Come and lay down. You've been working harder than I have and I want you in the bed beside me. I want to suck your cock. I never get tired of giving you a blowjob." And Jonas never got tired of getting one from her.

Jonas leaned over her, brushed a kiss across her lips, placed his hands through her blouse and held her full hard breasts. Then he leaned and sucked her taut nipple. "I'll be right back, someone's ringing the door bell, and they won't go away," he whispered and kissed her as he raised her short skirt and pulled her panties down and smelled them. She smiled opening her legs.

"Okay Jonas but when I wake I want your cock in my mouth or inside my pussy." Jonas chuckled because her words were beyond sexy and hot. He hated to leave her but as soon as he saw who was at the door, he'd be back and fucking Brooke as hard as he can.

"Okay. Hold your horses. I'm coming," Jonas yelled as he sauntered to the door. Jonas swung the door open, and standing in the doorway was Alex.

"Oh my God, Alex, you're here. How? When? Why?"

"It seems you forgot that you'd sent me and Max an invitation. He's flying in for the wedding on Saturday morning. He said that he couldn't make it earlier. And under no circumstances was I to take the children out of school. So all you have is me." Jonas grabbed Alex and pulled her inside the house. Then he reached for her bag and brought it in.

"You're not staying long are you?"

"Long enough, Jonas. It's not like it used to be. The children are older now."

"They haven't forgot me?" Jonas said pulling Alex into the living room over-looking the ocean.

"You have a wonderful view here."

"Just wait until I take you to the house I bought for Brooke." Alex aimed a closed smile at Jonas. It was a smile that said she was happy for him, but she wasn't happy to lose him. Alex turned to face Jonas.

"Where is this lucky woman?"

"She's sleeping. She stays up with me all night at the bar trying to get it ready, and she's studying for finals. Imagine that, and she's smart Alex. Just like you."

"I can't wait to meet her."

"Do you want coffee and toast?"

"I'll take an English muffin if you have one with coffee." Jonas turned and Alex followed him. "I can get the coffee going and you pop the muffin into the toaster." Alex stood at the coffeemaker and then she saw a shadow between the bushes. "Do you have a lawn man?"

"Yeah, but he doesn't come on Thursdays."

"I thought I saw a man about forty among the bushes." Jonas knew who it could be, but he wasn't sure. He didn't want to tell Alex anything because she wouldn't be there long just until Sunday and after that he'd move into his home in a gated community, and no one would know where to find him and Brooke.

Jonas didn't tell Alex and he didn't tell Brooke the day he was interviewing for positions in his bar that Mark Waterman, Brooke's ex had strolled into the bar. When Jonas glanced at him he didn't recognize him until he sat down at one of the tables under the pretense that he had sent an application for the manager's position.

"I'm not taking any more applications, or interviewing anyone else today. You will have to come back tomorrow," Jonas stated not looking up. He had been checking the inventory. When the man came up to the bar and stood in front of Jonas, Jonas raised his head. "Sorry but did you hear me?"

"I heard everything you said. But now I want you to hear me." Then it flashed through his mind that he'd seen this man before.

"I'm Mark." *What the fuck?* Jonas thought.

"I know who you are. What do you want?"

"I think you know what I want. Brooke."

"She's not merchandise where you shuffle her back and forth."

"Brooke's my merchandise."

"I think you've got everything wrong, Mark. Brooke is going to marry me and—"

"And I know. You're going to live happily ever after and fuck every day and have babies. I've heard that before with every man she meets and convinces him that she'll be with him for the rest of her life. It doesn't work that way. She's mine and you're not going to have her," Mark hissed. His nostrils flaring, his brow furrowed and his dark eyes staring through Jonas.

Jonas had seen that look before. It was the look of a predator and a killer. He'd seen that look when he returned from the war staring at him in the mirror, but he doubted that Mark had seen any combat. Not like him and the looked didn't scare him in the least.

"Jonas. Jonas," Alex said in a soft voice. Her voice had broken through his thoughts of Mark. He should have told Brooke, but he didn't want to upset her and he thought he could handle it. He'd been through hell, and what's another raindrop in an ocean?

"What's the matter? Are you taking your meds?"

"I'm taking them. I don't like when you ask me that, Alex. Why don't you tell me what's going on with you and Max."

They sat at the kitchen island with their coffee cups. Alex took a sip and glanced over at Jonas who stared out not looking at anything in particular, and then bringing his gaze into his cup. Alex knew something was bothering him but what could it be. He hadn't been in Miami long enough to get into trouble, or had he?

Trouble seemed to follow Jonas like buzzards followed half dead animals.

Alex leaned and placed her palm on the side of Jonas's face, caressed his chin, and then she turned his face to meet hers. He tried to lower his eyes but she knew him well. "Jonas you can tell me. What is it?"

"Brooke has an ex."

"When you say ex, do you mean an ex-husband?"

"No. Nothing like that. He was her boyfriend. She's never been married at least I don't think she has."

"Isn't that something you should find out first before you decide to marry someone?"

"I know all I need to know about her. I'm in love with her and that's all I need to know or want to know. No husband or boyfriend is going to change my feelings for Brooke. I know what kind of person she is. She's like you, Alex."

"For fuck's sake, Jonas. When are you going to grow up?" Alex snapped, not realizing how her voice affected Jonas. He pulled back from her hand.

"Don't talk to me like I'm a child. Some of Max is rubbing off on you. You never acted like that with me before. You were always encouraging me."

"We are both older and I have children to think about. You have children."

"They probably hate me because of Crystal, she probably told them something ugly about me."

"Crystal wouldn't do that. Now tell me about this man."

"His name is Mark."

"Mark came here, Jonas and you didn't tell me?" Alex and Jonas turned to see Brooke standing in the door way, her eyes wide, and her hands trembling at her side. Jonas rushed to Brooke placed his arms around her.

"Sit down, baby. It's going to be okay."

"How do you know?" Then she turned to glare at Alex with narrowed eyes. "Who is she? You let a stranger in. She could be working for Mark."

"Calm down, baby. Take my coffee." He handed her his cup. "This is Alex. My brother's wife. My best friend in the world." Brooke lowered her eyes and rubbed her palms together, up and down, in front of her face.

Alex watched the young girl. She thought Brooke was too young for Jonas, but she'd never tell him that. Who was she to say that Brooke wasn't his type or too young? It could have been said about her and

Max at first glance, but nothing could have been further from the truth. Alex and Max were made for each other.

"It's a pleasure to meet you Brooke. I hope we can be good friends." Brooke shook her head up and down and she didn't say a word. She stared ahead. Then she focused and turned her head and gazed at Alex.

Brooke narrowed her gaze. "You look like me. But you don't look older you look as if you're my age and I'm twenty."

"I'm twenty-six. Not much differences in our ages."

"You're beautiful, Alex." Brooke placed her palm on the side of Alex's face as if to check if she's real. Jonas watched the two women interact together and he felt relieved that there wasn't jealousy or animosity between them.

"So are you," Alex added with a warm inviting smile. Then Brooke looked over to Jonas sitting to her left. "I'm tired sweetheart, I don't want to sleep alone. Come to bed with me. You need sleep too." Brooke rose from the chair and stood behind him. Jonas watched Alex. Then Jonas rose up from the bar stools and held Brooke's hand. "Alex make yourself at home. There's a guest room with a bath in the back, if you need me to show you I'll be glad to, but after I get Brooke to sleep."

"I'll be fine, Jonas. Take care of Brooke and you, get some sleep." Alex stood and walked over to Jonas and kissed his cheek. He leaned in and hugged Alex. "I have to call the children and check on Max. You know how he is. He waits until the last minute and rushes home. In which case he'll probably make it to the wedding at the last minute, but he'll make it."

Alex watched as Jonas and Brooked trotted off kissing, in the direction of their bedroom. She thought how child like they both were. Jonas didn't need a child he had to take care of, he couldn't take care of himself. It had been Alex and Max seeing after Jonas.

# Chapter 12

After Jonas and Brooke disappeared, Alex made a call to Max. "Max are you going to make the opening of Jonas's bar?"

"I'm not sure baby. I have so many things to clear up, and you know what happens when I delegate, I still have to make sure that I check over everything."

"Then what's the point? You promised me that you would sell off your companies the last time. Now you've run away Jonas, and I have no one to help me with the children, or keep me sane in this desolate place."

"I don't want to argue with you, Alex. Especially about Jonas. You don't know how many companies I own and how difficult it is to downsize, liquidate, and sell off these damn companies." Max didn't like raising his voice to Alex. He was as much infuriated as Alex must have been because of his long stays away from her, and his children. "I'll have to lay-off thousands if I don't get this right. These men and women have families to think about."

"What about your family? What about me? I lay here every night and all I have is a picture of you. You pop in and fuck me on occasion. You don't have time to make love to me anymore."

"All I want to do is be with you, baby. Have your warm sexy body next to me at night. Nothing else. I need time. Give me time and I promise you that everything I said will come true. And as far as Jonas, he was getting too—"

"Too close to me. Is that why you sent him away?"

"I wanted to say that he was relying on you too much. For fuck's sake you're not his mother, Alex," Max argued.

"I think Jonas knows that better than any of us." Alex didn't want to admit that maybe Jonas should have left a long time ago, then all the craziness that happened wouldn't have put her and her family in jeopardy. She knew how much Jonas depended on her, and sooner than later he would tell her something that she didn't want to face—that he was in love with her, and she may have the same feelings for him.

Max was never around and Alex understood even if Max didn't, that 'you desire that which is close to you.' Jonas had been closer to her than Max lately, and Max had been her loving husband. The man she'd desired above all else. The man who knew her secret cravings and she knew Max's secret longings—to be shackled and beaten by her whenever he'd come home unsure of himself, and when he'd stayed away from her too many days and too many nights.

Then, Alex spent more time with Jonas, she and their children, more than she spent with Max. Alex had grown close to Jonas and Alex knew it, and perhaps Max did too. She feared Jonas had taken Max's place, that's why Alex needed Max home with her, and she'd been terrified that Jonas relished his role as a surrogate father and husband.

She'd been afraid that if Jonas called her for help, she would have defied Max's orders and gone to him. But now all Jonas wanted was to have the both of them at his wedding. The two people closest to him to share a wonderful time in his life, and maybe to cut ties with them the way a mother cuts ties with a loving son leaving home for the first time.

"I know I'm not his mother," Alex insisted. "But Jonas needs both of us to be with him at the most important time in his life. He needs that more now than at any time. He's fragile with you cutting the umbilical cord you created." There was silence that couldn't be interrupted because Max thought about what Alex had said, and he knew the truth when he'd heard it—he had caused most of Jonas's forbidden behaviors. He'd pulled strings from one coast to the other to get him out of all his mess. However, Max didn't know what to do. He'd been in a catch twenty-two. More like a fly caught in a spider's web. The more Max tried to distance himself from Jonas, the more he'd been drawn into Jonas's never ending saga of fuck-ups.

"You're there, Alex. You're where you want to be. Away from the solitude of the country and in the big city," Max's voice roared in an accusatory manner. He'd become the Master when speaking to Alex and she recognized that.

Alex assumed her submissive voice. "But I'm not with you, Max, and that's the only place I've wanted to be. With you lying next to me when I wake up in the mornings, and with you inside me after you've blindfolded, tied me up, used your crop on my ass, and sucked my nipples and clit raw. "

A long silence settled and filled their thoughts until Max said, "I'll be there for the opening of the bar and I'll stay for the wedding. Then I'm taking you home where you can chain me to the bed, flog me for not keeping my promises to you."

"I'll settle for handcuffing you to the bed, sucking your cock until you're ready to cum and not letting you cum." I want you to walk around with a hard shaft for at least two days and you can't touch yourself until I'm ready for you to cum."

"I knew you were a tease when I met you," Max said in a low seductive voice.

"You knew nothing of the sort. You made me a tease and everything else I am. I became what you wanted because I wanted you so much."

"I didn't know that," Max admitted. "Do you mean I could have done anything to you I wanted? Make you kiss my shoes, tied you up, and fucked you."

"You did that," Alex joked. "All except having me kiss your shoes. You kissed my heels remember as I ran one along your hard chest, after I flicked that heel on your nipple. You grabbed my shoe, pulled it off my feet, and then sucked my toes."

"Alex, I'm getting an erection. I can't work like that. You know you're the only woman I can get hard for. That's why I'll never let you go," Max whispered into the phone.

"I know, Max. I know." There was a bit of sadness in Alex's voice. She loved Max so much and never wanted to leave him, but she needed more than fly in fuck and fly out again. Max's routine had been, get satisfied, fuck, get his monthly beatings, fuck, and then he'd leave for another part of the world.

Max had gotten used to the predictable events of their lives, and Alex suspected that he'd never give up that part of his life. She wanted him to make love to her. Maybe his thoughts of lovemaking had been different from hers. Hell yes they were. She wanted him to bring her flowers, not a new gadget to tie her up and then bring her to orgasm. She wanted to wake up in the mornings and not find an empty space next to her. Not another a note on his pillow telling her what he wanted her to do to him the next time he came home. She wanted that now. She wanted him with her now.

"Alex. Alex?"

"Yes, Max."

"I'll try to make the opening, if not, I promise you I'll be at the wedding on Saturday." Alex knew if it were at all possible, Max would keep his promise. He'd kept most of his promises to her and because of that, she overlooked the little things he'd promised, and didn't keep.

"Jonas is going on his honeymoon on Sunday. They're flying out you know. Did you remember to have the extra jet ready?"

"Don't worry. All that's taken care of." It was a relief to Alex to hear that Max's voice had changed. Maybe it was because Jonas would be getting married and he didn't have to worry about him for a while.

"We have to stay here to help close the house and hand the rental office the key. He's only staying a week because of the bar and we'll have the house to ourselves. There's a pool and the beach. Who knows what we can do that Sunday night," Alex said, her voice low, sexy and inviting.

"I know what I can do. Now I have to go. I've held up my meetings long enough. If you want me there then let me go, baby. Oh I forgot to ask. What kind of woman is Jonas marrying?"

"Young and pretty. I'll send a picture of her, and the bar, later."

"I hope not too young. The first young pretty thing was underage. I hope he checked her age. I don't have time or money to convince parents not to put him in jail. I have to go now, baby. I'll fly in and check on our children, and then I'll meet you on opening night."

"Kiss the children for me." Alex hit the button and held the phone to her chest. Then she sighed and picked up her purse, placed the phone in it, and trotted down the hall to the spare bedroom. When she opened the door, it was a wonderful room full of light and the sound of the ocean. Which was good because she'd planned on lying in the sun and going for a swim in his pool and maybe skinny dipping in the ocean when Max arrived.

When Alex glanced up, Jonas stood leaning in the doorway. "Is everything okay?"

"Did you sleep?" Alex asked.

"Only a little. I closed my eyes if that's what you mean? I don't need that much sleep. I'm like your husband. Well almost like him." Jonas walked into the room as Alex placed her clothing in the drawer and hung up a few things. He sat on the bed and watched her. "You and Brooke do look alike."

"I hope that wasn't on purpose."

"What do you mean, Alex?"

"I think you know what I mean, Jonas." Jonas lowered his head and then raised it to meet Alex's eyes.

"No. I didn't plan to meet someone who looked like you. That was the furthest thing from my mind. It just happened. A fortuitous meeting. It wasn't planned if you think that. I'll tell you about it later. Do you want to come with me to the club? Maybe look around and give me pointers."

"Don't you want to wait until Brooke wakes up?"

"She'll be alright. She needs to rest because she has another final Friday evening."

"The night of your opening?"

"I have you and Max coming to celebrate with me, that's all I need. You and Max and soon I'll have my family, and I won't have to depend on Max. But you, I will always need." Jonas rose from the bed and held out his hand and Alex placed her palm inside his after aiming a closed warm smile his way.

# Chapter 13

"You have a great place here, Jonas. I never thought you'd find something like this. It suits you just fine." Alex sauntered through the tables and booths, walked up to the bar, placed her hand down and walked the length of it, turned to face Jonas. You actually found something that you can do that's better than dealing with those Bondage Clubs."

Looking down at her with a broad smile, "Those bondage clubs brought in a lot of money. This won't be as lucrative—"

"But you'll be able to sleep at night in your own bed with your wife."

"Now that's a thought. A good one at that."

Jonas and Alex sat on the barstool next to each other in front of a large mirror, and when Alex glanced around the room there were flat televisions in every corner and off to the sides. "People like to watch television and drink. It's like being at home only you're not lonely, you have people to share your life with, if just for a few hours."

Alex and Jonas's eyes locked on each other. Each one saw something different. Alex saw Max. Jonas had Max's face, smile, and eyes. Identical twins and few could tell them apart. But Alex could when Jonas smiled at her.

Jonas saw Alex. Beautiful, young, and self-confident. A woman he'd kill for, but couldn't touch or have. He had to settle for the next best thing—a real woman he could have, and not a fantasy. He couldn't fuck a fantasy—only in his dreams. When he looked down at Brooke's face when he was fucking her, he thought of Alex. When he'd asked Brooke to tie him up and sit on his cock, he thought of Alex. When he'd handcuffed Brooke, and had her face down on his bed, her ass in the air, he took her from behind, and thought of Alex.

"Jonas. Where are you going on your honeymoon?"

Jonas turned to Alex after staring in the mirror thinking about her. "We're flying out to Hawaii. Max said we could use one of his jets."

"When I talked to him he did say that he had taken care of everything. I thought he'd gotten rid of those company jets," Alex said.

"He kept two and one of those small planes. One jet as a standby, and one for the company. The plane is for travel over a short distance, and only when he needs to travel a few miles. You know Max always keeps a spare." Alex narrowed her gaze at Jonas. "I didn't mean that, what I meant, Alex, well... he'd never look at another woman. If I had a woman like you, I'd never want or look at another either."

Alex hopped off the bar. "I think I want to make myself a drink. She strolled around the bar, reached, and offered a beer to Jonas. Then she poured herself a vodka shot and drank it, then sucked the lime.

When she looked up she saw a tall man in a light weight suit standing inside the bar. Then she heard him say, "While you're sucking on that lime what about coming home tonight and suck my cock the way you used to before you met Blackstone."

Jonas jumped from the seat turned to face the man who had made those crude remarks to Alex. Then Jonas's long legs strode in his direction, and met the man half way. He stood eye to eye with Jonas. "She's not Brooke and I want you to apologize to her," Jonas growled.

"He doesn't have to, Jonas." When Mark heard Alex speak he realized that Jonas had told the truth. Mark continued walking in the direction to the bar. Jonas with a furrowed brow, and long strides, marched alongside Mark whispering something to him that Alex didn't here. Whatever it was, it didn't deter Mark from reaching the bar to get a better look at the woman standing behind it.

"I'm closed," Jonas said turning to face Mark who leaned on the bar to get a better look at Alex.

Mark slanted his head to the side. "You look like Brooke. I thought you were her. You have the same hair. Same face and damn but you're beautiful. You're older than her but you can't really tell." Then he turned to Jonas. "You're fucking both of them? That's kind of sick isn't it? Fuck two woman who look alike."

Mark turned back to face Alex as he leaned forward. "Did he tell you what kind of woman my Brooke is? I created her to service me, and then he comes along and she leaves me for this. She's my Dominant," Marks said his voice filled with pain.

Alex turned to Jonas. "I think we should close the doors and go, Jonas. I haven't eaten today."

"Would you go with me to dinner? I know a great restaurant," Mark stated leaning back crossing his arms over his chest, his eyes locked with Alex. Alex didn't waver on her stare, but Mark lowered his eyes submissive to her. Mark knew immediately that she was a dominant. She had been a dominant to every man who wanted her but Max. They'd shared that role equally.

"No thank you."

"Why not? I can give you as much as he's giving you. I'm a great looking guy, but I'm a little lonely. I probably won't talk about anyone but Brooke. I'll pay you to listen to me cry my heart out over her. He took her from me. Did he tell you that? And who did he steal you from?"

"Don't say one more word, Mark. This is my sister-in-law and you're drunk. Go home and forget Brooke. She's with me now. She's not going back to you—ever."

Mark turned after he'd taken one more look at Alex and aimed a smile her way. "Beautiful. If you ever need a sub, I'm your man beautiful lady." And Mark stumbled out of the bar, into a limo after tightening his jaw, narrowing his glance, and shaking his head at Jonas.

"What the fuck was that about, Jonas?"

"Let's get out of here. I'll tell you on the ride home."

Jonas locked up, and they climbed into the corvette, he turned the music down low and told Alex about how he met Brooke. He told her about her leaving Mark and why. He told Alex how Mark watched men make love to Brooke, and that she had met him when she was seventeen and had been married to him when she turned eighteen, and that she ran away and got a divorce from him and he's married now, but he can't let her go even when she'd broken it off with him several times.

When Mark found her again, she had been homeless and went back to him for fear she'd have to live on the street. He bought her a house, sent her to college, but he kept bringing men to her, and he'd said that he'd never let her go.

As Jonas pulled into the driveway and turned off the motor, Alex sat quietly with her eyes closed. She couldn't believe how Jonas had managed to get himself into this. "I have to tell Max," she said.

Jonas reached for her arm. "Don't. Please don't."

"You know what happens every time I keep things from Max. It doesn't end well."

"It will be okay. We're moving from here, out of this house, and he won't be able to find her."

"You have a business. How are you going to deal with that?"

"He doesn't want me. He wants Brooke."

"Can't you see what's going on? Mark, that's his name, he's a desperate man and desperate men in love will do anything. Brooke's his dominant. She has to take responsibility for this too. Take Max for example. Don't you realize that he will never let me go? He has done any and everything to keep me. Max loves me, and he has a deep need that goes beyond me being his wife. He hungers for what I do to and for him. If Max thinks anyone will take me from him, he becomes almost dangerous. You know it. I've seen men like him. Do you remember Robert?"

How could Jonas forget Robert? But he tried.

"I've tried to forget Robert. He tried to come in between me and Max. Do you remember what happened to him?"

"But you can't think that Max would have anything to do with that?"

"I don't know, Jonas, but that man has the same look in his eyes as a man who's desperate not to lose something precious. I can tell you for sure, he's into all kinds of sexual games that he probably plays with Brooke. How do you know she's not playing a game with you to make Mark jealous?"

"Let's get out of the car. It's making me nervous. I can't stand being in confined places too long, Alex." After walking out the car, and Jonas opening the door to the house for Alex, she stopped in the foyer turned and glared at him.

"You didn't answer me, Jonas. She could be playing games with you."

"She isn't. She loves me. I can feel it. She makes me happy and I want to live again. I don't know what I'll do if something happens to her." Alex glanced down because Jonas had a tight grip on her arm, but when he realized that he was hurting her, he dropped his hands.

"I'll get us something to eat," Alex suggested.

"I can order something, Alex."

"I know how to cook, Jonas. You need something hot. I can make you some soup. "Do you have some chicken?"

"Yeah. Left over cold chicken."

"Perfect. What time are Brooke's classes over?"

"I don't know I never asked her."

"You should find out. And you should warn her about Mark."

"I will, Alex. I will. Just do one thing for me. Help Brooke dress for our wedding. She invited her sister, mother, and father and although I arranged for a suite for them and plane tickets, car to meet them at the airport, they said they would go to the hotel and wouldn't be here until it was time for the wedding. Even her sister refused to be her maid of honor."

Alex studied what Jonas had revealed to her and something was weird about the whole thing. About her family in particular.

All of it bothered Alex.

"I'll do my best to make your wedding a happy occasion. I promise you. Now let me get something prepared for us to eat. I'm hungry if you're not and I don't want pizza. I've eaten enough of that with the kids."

Jonas made a few calls to make sure the manager he'd just hired would take care of everything when he was on his honeymoon. He'd wanted to marry at the bar, but he didn't want everyone at his wedding. He thought it would be a solemn occasion and he didn't want strangers sharing his precious day. And he thought Mark would cause problems. It would just be Jonas's family, and Brooke's family, and that suited him just fine.

After his calls he became hungry and decided to see if Alex had finished the soup. He could smell it before he entered the kitchen. It was a chicken soup with noodles. He stopped in his tracks because that was his last memories of his mother, and how she would cook that soup for him when he was sick. All Alex needed was to make some lemon cakes and he'd be on cloud nine.

Jonas tipped up behind Alex and because she had focused on cooking, she didn't hear him. He placed his hands on her slim waist, and she jumped. "You shouldn't do that with something hot in my hands. Alex cautioned Jonas. "Here taste it. You're nothing but a little boy." Jonas smiled and took a sip of the soup.

"It taste wonderful. What is that perfume you're wearing? I like that smell. I want to get some for Brooke.

"Brooke can buy her own perfume, Jonas." Alex and Jonas turned to see Brooke standing watching Jonas hold Alex around the waist, and leaning in smelling her hair and neck. Alex didn't noticed it because she was busy adding more seasoning to the soup.

"Hi Brooke. I made enough soup for you." Brooke looked at her and then looked at Jonas.

"I need to speak to you," Brooke said to Jonas in a commanding strong voice. A voice that wasn't in keeping with her soft low voice Alex had first heard. She stared at Alex when she turned to face her.

When Jonas didn't move quick enough Brooke said, "Now, Jonas. Don't keep me waiting." Alex knew the sound of a Dominant. How could she miss those cues? She knew that well. She had been one for Max. However, being married to him, and how they shared their roles of dominant and submissive, wasn't necessary anymore to prove who the dominant in their relationship was. They'd come to an understanding with each other.

However, Jonas and Brooke's relationship was new, and it was apparent that Brooke had become the dominant even as Jonas was once considered to be a Master and the Alpha in his previous relationships.

Alex knew Jonas was a willing participant and he'd been just the type to give in to Brooke. It was Brooke the one who controlled Mark too. The things that Jonas had told Alex about how he'd met Brooke, the men she'd claimed that Mark wanted her to fuck, and it suddenly dawned on Alex that Brooke was controlling both men. They were there to service her wanton desires.

There was no way Alex could tell Jonas. He had to find out on his own because Alex knew one thing— they always shoot the messenger.

# Chapter 14

When Alex had placed the table setting on the bar for the three of them, poured the soup into a large bowl, placed the ladle inside the soup tureen, she set French sour dough bread on a plate in front of the setting. Proud of herself and ready to smooth things over between her and Brooke by assuring her that she wasn't the enemy, and would be her sister-in-law, and they could become good friends if Brooke gave her a chance.

Alex strolled down the hall, turned to face Jonas's door, raising her hands to knock, to tell them to come out and eat, the soup was ready. She came to a sudden stop in front of the door because it was ajar and she could see Brook. Brooke stood her legs wide, naked, with only high heels on as she held a leather flogger in her hand. When Alex caught her breath ready to open her mouth, she saw Jonas with his wrists and feet tied to the bed naked and he too was naked, face down, his arms and legs splayed.

"You're not to touch another woman but me. Say it, Jonas," Brooke ranted as she hit him twice on each ass cheek.

"Master, I'm not to touch another woman but you." And with the leather crop in her hand, she stood over him, lashing him several times on his buttocks. "When I take these handcuffs off, I want you to eat my pussy, and don't wipe your mouth until I tell you to. I want that slut you call Alex to know that you're my property, and that she should never think that she could own you, because I own you, Jonas Blackstone." And Brooke beat Jonas until she broke skin. As he lay there she didn't sooth his behind, or give him anything to ease his pain. "Now get up and get that soup that slut made and bring it to me. I'm going to take a shower."

After what Alex saw, she shuddered, turned before Jonas could see her, and headed back to the kitchen shaking. If Brooke continued with those kinds of beatings, Jonas would be broken. If the war hadn't completely wiped him out, the woman of his dreams would, and she would be a nightmare to him and everyone he'd loved.

Alex knew how Mark appeared to be damaged and she knew it was at Brooke's hands. This young woman had taken control of two very handsome rich men and if Alex didn't do something, she would ruin Jonas the same way she'd probably ruined Mark. Jonas had been broken by war and life and now this woman had come in to finish him off.

When Jonas finally ambled into the kitchen, Alex glared at him and said, "Do you know what you're doing?" Alex filled the bowl with soup then watched Jonas who never glanced up at her.

He raised his eyes but not his head. His breath shallow, his hands shaky after placing a bowl of hot soup on a tray. "What do you mean?"

"I think you know what I mean, Jonas. You're no longer the Master or Dominant you're a submissive. You've given away your control to Brooke. You just met her."

"What were you doing? Snooping around, spying on me? What did you see?" Alex hadn't seen much. Was there more she'd missed? She'd felt thankful that she didn't catch all that act. "Why are you judging me? You control Max," he barked.

"It's not the same thing, Jonas. You don't have children and you're not married to her. You have no history with her. Max and I have a history, we love each other, we share control and we're not in public using our power over the other person. Brooke wanted me to see that she controlled you and you fell for her shit. When you have power you don't need to prove it."

"Brooke is young. With my tutelage she'll be better."

"I don't think you can teach her anything. She looked like she could teach you a few things. You know nothing about her and from what I see it's one way. Her way. Did you at least google her." By the look on Jonas's face he did nothing. "You should have at least found out something about her. She could be a man."

Jonas chuckled, "I think I would know if she was a man or not."

"I hope so, but the way you're behaving, I wonder," Alex said as Jonas headed for the doorway.

Then Jonas turned and admitted. "Brooke makes me feel. When she flogged me, a cloud lifted. She's all I want." Jonas took a step and then turned back to Alex. "You're taken."

"What did you say, Jonas?" Alex narrowed her eyes.

"You heard me. Don't act so surprised," he argued.

"Don't say that Jonas. Don't ever say that to me again."

"It's true. What the fuck do you want? For me to lie to you. I'm trying to find someone like you. She looks like you. Didn't that give you a hint about how I felt about you? So now I have. Now wish me well." And Jonas walked out of the room carrying the cold soup.

Alex tried to compose herself. She was shaking all over thinking about what Jonas had said to her. Where the fuck was Max? Can't he be with her sometimes when she needed him? She needed him now more than ever and so did Jonas.

Alex knew Jonas had made the biggest mistake of his life, and there was no way that young woman was anything like her. Maybe in looks, but that was where the similarities began and ended.

Rushing to find her phone she didn't know where Max was, but she had to talk to him. He had to make it tomorrow. She texted him and then left a message with his answering service. It wasn't an emergency, and Alex didn't want to leave a message where Max would be upset and not go home first to check on the children, so she ended the call.

Alex threw her phone down. When she glanced up, Brooke had been looking at her, studying her. "What's the matter? Can't control your submissive?"

"For your information he's not my submissive, he's my husband."

"What is the difference?"

"If you don't know the difference, I can't tell you." Brooke reached for her backpack and flung it across her shoulder and turned to leave. "Did Jonas tell you that your ex came into the bar?" Alex taunted.

"Why would he tell me that? I have that under control."

"Like you have Jonas under your control."

"Precisely. Now if you don't have anything else to tell me, I'm going to be late for class."

"I don't have anything to tell you, but I will say one thing. If you do anything to fuck with Jonas in any way, including string him alone and take another man to bed with Jonas, you will have me to deal with."

Brooke stared at Alex, tightened her jaw, twisted her mouth and said, "I think you're in love with Jonas. We could make it a threesome maybe foursome if his brother is in with this." Then Brooke laughed. "I can tell by the look in your eyes and your expression when I suggested that Max join us, you really are in love with Jonas, and you don't want to share either one of those handsome brothers. What will your husband say when he discovers the truth about you."

"There isn't anything to discover about me and Jonas," Alex objected.

"You mean you haven't taken him to bed and made him wear a collar, chains, and made him kiss your feet, and fucked him with your favorite sex toys yet? Well I have, and you haven't lived until you have a man like Jonas at your beck and call ready to do anything for you." Brooke raised her chin and her head fell back as she laughed and laughed at Alex.

"Don't get me wrong. We are both alike. I can tell. You don't want to share and I don't want to share Jonas with you. Do you understand me?"

Alex sauntered around the island to where Brooke stood. Then she leaned and in a low whisper confessed.

"I understand you perfectly. But don't think we're alike. You haven't lived long enough to know what I'm like or what I'm capable of. You can't begin to fathom how I can control men. You will never have Jonas completely because I won't allow that. Get that in your head. You can fuck around with Mark because he's weak and loves you, but Jonas will never love anyone but me." And Alex aimed at Brooke a closed overconfident smile.

That statement even surprised Alex. She couldn't believe she'd allowed Brooke to goad her into expressing her innermost thoughts about Jonas. She never admitted that to anyone. Not even Jonas. Brooke's face changed from shrewd and arrogant to sour and bitter.

"I knew what you were when I first met you. You're nothing but a slut."

"Yes I guess I am, and perhaps a better slut than you, but I'm afraid you have me on those sex toys. I've never had those fantasies about Jonas." Now after the air cleared and oxygen got to Alex's brain, she realized that she should have never said that and to Brooke. She tried to correct it but she didn't think Brooke would believe her when she said, "Jonas is like a brother to me."

"The fuck he is," Brooke grumbled, stormed out the back door, and walked down around the stone path to climb into her new white Mercedes Jonas had bought her for a wedding present.

# Chapter 15

When Alex hurried anxiously around Miami looking for a business that could provide flowers, and all sort of decorations, to decorate the house, the outside garden and patio, and the bar for Jonas and Brooke's wedding. She opened the door for the caterers to bring in the food and drinks, made sure the cleaning crew had done their jobs correctly to her specifications, nevertheless, Brooke had been conveniently absent since yesterday. She hadn't bothered to come home last night, or go to the club to help Jonas with the opening of his bar.

Alex had been there to help at the last minute. Jonas had called her and said that he needed someone and he didn't anticipate that the place would be so busy and since she'd been a waitress, Alex had agreed to go and help out.

"Where's Brooke?" Alex had said to Jonas.

"She said that she had something important to do and that she would be home later." Alex didn't ask any more questions, however, when Jonas slogged in early in the morning after she'd called an Uber to take her home, and missed a call from Max, she never bothered Jonas. She knew she couldn't count on Brooke helping her because she'd gotten the feeling from Brooke yesterday, that she didn't want to be around her, and Alex felt the same way.

If she didn't ever see Brooke again it would be too soon. However, she wouldn't be that lucky because Brooke had to return sometime because today was her wedding. And Alex had been certain she wouldn't miss that.

Alex stood on the ladder and placed the last lanterns on the beams of the outdoor patio trying to forget the argument she'd had with Brooke.

Standing below the ladder she looked down to see Jonas. "Thank you, Alex. I don't know what I'd do without you." She handed him her palm as he helped her down the ladder. When she stood looking up at his handsome tired face, she commented, "You look tired Jonas. When did you get in?"

"About two hours ago. I fell on the bed and I just woke. I'm sorry I wasn't any good to help out. Since Max didn't make it last night, and the wedding only a few hours away, do you think Max will get here on time? He never disappointed me before. Last night was the first time. The manager and his friends gave me a great bachelor party after we'd closed down and after you left. You know I've never had one before."

"Where was Brooke through all of this? I know you said she had classes and classes don't last all night. Shouldn't she be here now? It's not my wedding."

"She texted me and said that she was staying at a friend's house and that she would be home in time for the wedding."

"That was good of her. I know it's a small wedding just for your family and hers, but shouldn't she have been here sometime? Maybe just to approve of the cake."

"When she text me, I told her there wasn't much to do because you'd taken care of everything. The caterers brought in the food and cake and liquor, I see," Jonas said as he turned and glanced around the house. "In an hour I'll be a married man. Aren't you happy for me?"

Alex turned around and walked back into the house. Jonas walked behind her and stood looking at her as she pretended to arrange the platter of food. He'd wished it was Alex the one he'd marry, but then that was insane, he thought. So he dismissed that from his mind. "Alex, you don't like Brooke. I wished you two had gotten to know each other, you would love her like I do. She's not what you think."

*Brooke is exactly who and what I think she is*, Alex thought, as she stared blankly at the wedding cake. "Isn't this a beautiful cake? I picked it out and I don't know if Brooke would like it but that's too bad. She should have been here." And Alex marched away, but didn't get far before Jonas reached for her wrist and brought her around to face him.

"What is it, Alex? I've never seen you like this. Can't you be happy for me? You have been mean with everyone. I can understand you being short and sour with me, but not Brooke."

"Who told you that I didn't like her? Have I given you any reason to think otherwise?"

Then Alex's phone rang and she reached inside her pants. She looked at her IPhone and turned. "It's Max and I have to take this now."

"I'm going to take a shower and you need to do the same. We don't have much time."

"This isn't my wedding. Remember. When is Brooke getting here?" Jonas had gone when Alex answered.

"Max. When are you coming? I can't take any more of this. I need you here with me. I have so much to tell you about Jonas and that woman he's marrying."

"I thought you were happy that he was finally out of my hair and someone else would be responsible for him."

"That was until I had a chance to meet and talk to her."

"Look baby. That isn't your responsibility any more. It's time you stopped worrying over Jonas and start with me. I'm sorry I couldn't make it last night, but it was worth it. I waited until I knew that I was getting the right price for my hotel in Seattle. I'm home now and I will reach there within a half an hour. Oh, I forgot to tell you that my jet had to be serviced and since I'd offered Jonas the other jet, I'm flying myself in one of my smaller planes."

"Are you sure that's a good idea."

"It's the best one I have now because I'm in the air now and I'll make it there for the wedding."

"You might make it before the bride."

"What are you talking about, Alex?"

"I'll tell you when you get here. Love you, Max. I have to shower and get dressed." And they disconnected the call. Alex hopped into the shower and dressed, put her hair up into a bun and hurried out of the room after placing very little makeup on and swiping pink lipstick on her lips.

· · · ·

THE CHIME RANG FROM the Ring camera and Alex realized that they would have guest in a few minutes, and Brooke hadn't arrived yet. Alex checked around to see if everything looked okay and was ready whenever the bride arrived. She looked in the garden and the flowers were fresh and hadn't wilted on the gazebo facing the few chairs arranged to look as if more people were attending. When Alex glanced through the large windows that anchored the door, a limo had arrived, and four people were climbing out of the car.

Alex sauntered to the door and opened it before they had a chance to ring the bell. "Please come in." The couple were in their fifties and according to their clothes they were just ordinary people. Not rich and not poor. The man was a handsome man with mingled grey hair and his wife short and bone thin with a tanned complexion. She may have been a beauty like Brooke when she was twenty, but she looked older and smelled of cigarettes.

"We're Brooke's parents. She did tell you about us," the mother gushed. Alex aimed a warm smile their way and shook their hands.

"Yes, she did talk fondly about all of you. I'm Mrs. Blackstone—"

"You're not Jonas's ex-wife are you?" The young girl interrupted.

"No. I'm his sister-in-law. My husband is the best man, and he'll be here later. He's flying down."

"In his own plane?" The young boy of sixteen asked Alex.

"See. Brooke always finds men that have money. He does have money?" The girl of fourteen or fifteen questioned.

"You ask too many questions," the boy said.

"Please come in and have a seat until the minister gets here and Brooke." They walked in to the living room where the tables were set up with all kinds of food.

"Where's Brooke? The father asked.

"She isn't here yet."

"I told Jonas when we met that he would have to treat her with a firm hand. If you know what I mean." Alex glanced over at him and then her eyes wandered to where Jonas stood dressed in his black tux.

"You look handsome, Mr. Blackstone," Brooke's mother said. "Doesn't he?" The daughter sidled up to Jonas and looked up and met his eyes as Alex watched the brazen young girl flirt with Jonas. Jonas gave out a nervous grin.

"I wish I was marrying him," the girl boasted.

Moving away and standing next to Alex, Jonas said, "Call me Jonas. If you're wondering where Brooke is she just text me and said that she was turning the corner." Then the bell rang. "Excuse me." Jonas hurried out of the room happy to get away from that group. He opened the door to greet the minister.

Before the minister could say a word, Brooke tore past him not acknowledging Jonas or stopping to kiss him. Stopping in the doorway, Brooke smiled. "Hi everyone. I'm here. I bet you thought I wouldn't make it." Then she turned to Alex. "I need you to help me get into my dress." The dress had been delivered yesterday and Alex had hung it in the closet. It was a long plain off white dress cut low in front.

Alex glared at Brooke. Of all the people to help her why didn't she ask her mother? Since she'd done that in front of her family and Jonas, Alex didn't want to appear insensitive, so she said, "Of course I'll help." Brooke turned and rushed into the room and Alex strolled behind her. When the door closed, Alex turned and glared at her.

"You know I did this for Jonas. And why are you asking me to help you? I can't stand you. I've been working in here to make your wedding successful, and you don't give a fuck about any of this. Not even Jonas."

"I guess you're right about one thing. I don't give a fuck. But I give a fuck about fucking and so do you. You want to fuck him," Brooke said as she stripped down and entered the shower. Alex reached for the dress and passed her palms over it. What a beautiful gown and to have someone that ugly wear it.

Brooke stepped out of the shower wearing a towel drying her hair. Then she dropped it and pranced in front of Alex. "I bet you used to look like me. But I bet after you had children it did something to your body. Stretch marks I bet. I'm never going to have that because I don't plan on having children."

"Did you tell Jonas?"

"Hand me my dress." Alex handed it to her. "Now zip me up."

"You're great at giving orders aren't you?"

"As a matter of fact I'm the best at getting men to do what I want." Alex zipped Brooke up.

"How did you fool Jonas into falling for your shit?"

"Men are weak. Jonas is weak. I have a thing for weak men. And you? How did you get your husband to marry you?"

"This is not about me. It's about you and Jonas. I'll never tell you anything about my relationship with my husband."

"Oh yeah. Jonas told me all about Max and how you met him. I think it's hilarious. And you have the nerve to question me about Jonas." Brooke turned to face Alex after she'd placed her shoes on her feet.

"Aren't you going to wear underwear?"

"I don't need any because I want to take Jonas in the room the minute we marry and let him eat my pussy. Now what do you think?"

"I think you've lost your mind...If you've ever had any."

"Well let me tell you what I think. You are jealous and wished he'd go down on you. Haven't you ever fantasized what it would be like to have a threesome with Max and Jonas? If you haven't, I have."

When Brooke turned to look in the mirror, Alex had her hand to Brooke's throat. "Let me tell you one thing, I don't give a fuck what you do with Jonas and who he let fuck you, but if you ever think you will fuck around with my husband, I will kill you."

Brooke stared into Alex's fiery amber eyes and she raised her hand and peeled Alex's hand from around her throat. "I will kill—"

The door opened and Jonas said, "Who are you going to kill, Alex?"

"I was just telling Brooke that I will kill her with kindness if she treats my favorite brother-in-law the way he deserve to be treated. Didn't I Brooke?"

"Yes, Alex did say that I should be good to you. I planned on being everything you want and then some." Brooke walked over to Jonas and kissed his lips and then unzipped his dress pants and placed her hand inside his boxers to jerk him off. Jonas's eyes closed as she wrapped her fist around Jonas's wet cock.

"I think I should go before we have to have the ceremony in the bedroom," Alex said passing the couple with Brooke eyeing her as she stepped to the door. "Don't you have to go Jonas? I'll wait outside for Brooke.

# Chapter 16

It had been a small beautiful wedding, Brooke and Jonas exchanged vows, and looked wonderful together. The perfect handsome man and beautiful young bride. Vogue magazine couldn't have captured a more handsome couple standing against a backdrop of ocean waves, the sun setting, colorful flowers, Brooke's mother crying with happiness, and then there's Alex unhappy trying to smile if only to make Jonas feel better. She wondered what happened to Max as did Jonas.

Brooke acted as if she loved Jonas, and for his and Alex's sake, she hoped Brooke did. No one would have known their secrets but Alex, but from Alex's observation Brooke's family knew more than they were letting on.

Jonas's best man hadn't made it yet and he felt downhearted. After the ceremony, Jonas strode up to Alex sitting in a corner, she'd been on her feet the entire day, and finally gave in to exhaustion. When Jonas discovered her sitting alone, while everyone around drank and ate, Alex had been staring at her phone all evening.

"What happened to Max? He promised me that he'd be my best man. I counted on him being here. I just thought if he'd been to my first marriage, then I would have had more luck."

"You can't depend on luck and Max to make a marriage work, Jonas. You need to find the right woman for you."

"What are you trying to say, Alex that Brooke's not the right woman?" Jonas's jaw tightened and his eyes glowed in anger at Alex.

"That's not for me to say. I didn't say that, Jonas." She didn't say it but she sure as hell meant just that. Alex reached to touch Jonas's hand and he pulled it away.

"You're damn right. You never wanted me with her. You thought that all the attention would be taken away from you." Jonas's words and voice were harsh, breathless, and angry.

"You're drunk, Jonas. Go find your wife."

"I'm not drunk. If I had met you instead of Max, I wouldn't have all this shit running around my head. I don't know what happened to her. I think she's next door."

"What's next door?"

"That's where she used to live with Mark."

"Do you mean to tell me that Mark is in that house, and you think that Brooke is over there with him?"

As Alex and Jonas talked with Jonas taking a sip of liquor and looking in the direction of Mark's home, Brooke's father and mother walked over.

"We're going to leave now, Jonas. Tell Brooke we're leaving early in the morning and there's no need to bother coming by the hotel because we have an early morning flight back to Georgia. When you and Brooke move into your mansion, then we'll be back to spend some time with her," Brooke's father said. Alex noticed that he didn't inquire where she'd disappeared to right after the wedding.

The two teenagers said goodbye and they stepped into Jonas's rented limo after their parents, and it took off with Jonas and Alex staring, and then eyeing each other. When the car disappeared from the driveway, Alex snapped. "You're buying a mansion, Jonas? I didn't know that?"

"I don't have to tell you everything, Alex. I'm married now, and I think that's between me and my wife. Where is she?"

"Isn't she your wife? Why are you asking me? Besides, I think you know." Alex watched Jonas slip into a submissive, heartbroken man. This wasn't half the man she'd seen in New York. He'd been the Master. She reached for Jonas and brought him into her arms.

Holding on to Alex, he confessed, "Alex. I don't know what to do. I think she's with Mark. Maybe I can't give her what she needs?"

"Let's face it, Jonas, can anyone give the ones we love everything they need?"

"No, Alex, you're right. You couldn't give me what I needed." Alex took the glass away.

"You're drunk and tired. You haven't had any rest. Go to bed I'll find Brooke and bring her here."

It appeared that all Alex ever did was take care of Jonas. When was that going to end? She thought as she traipsed around the path leading to the sprawling ranch style home. When she walked to the patio doors, she could see two figures. Both were naked and the man was on his knees wearing a collar, and from the back she saw Brooke standing tall with black leather, boots with spiked heels. In her hand she held a chain that held the collar, and she had a crop in her hands. With the spiked-heel of her boot, tracing down his spine, stopping at his hole, she used the crop to give him one hard lash, as she ground her heel, teasing his tight ring of muscles, with her spiked-heel tunneling into it.

On the couch next to Mark and Brooke laid a cock's cage and butt plug. Mark had been

There were moans of pleasure coming from him as Mark asked her to impale his balls. "I don't need them anyway," he moaned as he craned his head to look around at Brooke.

Alex couldn't hold her anger, "What the fuck Brooke? Have you lost your mind?" Alex questioned. "You know what you're doing?" Brooke took her foot and pushed Mark down to the floor.

"I know exactly what I'm doing. Why don't you go back to Jonas? Keep him company until I get back. I don't care. Suck his dick. Do something because I'm busy and I'm not leaving Mark until I've disciplined him."

There was no talking to her. There was no way to reason with Brooke. Brooke thought she knew how to discipline men who had been in love with her, she thought she knew men, she thought she could move from one man to the other without any consequences, toy with them, humiliate them, but she knew very little about men, Alex thought.

"I have nothing else to say. But I warned you. If you hurt Jonas, I will—"

"I heard you, now leave us." There was a coldness in Brooke's voice. She fooled Jonas because he'd always been trusting, and a fool for a beautiful ass.

Alex walked away and when she returned to the empty house except for her and Jonas, she found a bottle of vodka, and poured herself one drink. On her way to the extra bedroom, she passed and looked in on Jonas.

He'd fallen asleep across his bed. It was better that he sleep than to know about what his blushing bride had been up to with her ex. Jonas had been too tired what with staying up working at his bar, fucking and being abused by Brooke, the drinking and wedding which had taken a toll on him.

If Jonas hadn't had his plate full, Brooke wouldn't have been next door. She would have been working her trade on Jonas, and like Mark he would have enjoyed every minute of it. But it was something about Brooke that let Alex know that she wouldn't be satisfied with one or two men even. She appeared to have an addiction and everyone knows addicts can't help themselves. Maybe that's what Jonas knew, Alex thought. In any case that was between Jonas and his blushing bride.

Alex had been tired too with all the work left for her to do. She'd managed to undress and glance at her phone. Still nothing from Max. How could he let her down? No. How could he let Jonas down? She'd become used to it, but not anymore. She'll put her foot down and take control of her husband this time.

In a way Alex admired Brooke, and in another way, she loathed her for what she'd done to Jonas. Those were Alex's last thoughts as she lay in the bed thinking of Max and imagining about Jonas's life, how he could have been if he hadn't gone to Afghanistan, and if he'd found the right woman for him.

• • • •

WHEN ALEX OPENED HER eyes the sun was rising and peeking through the shutters, then she heard something pop like a firecracker. She sat up in bed, blinked her eyes listening for another sound but nothing came. Alex waited a few more minutes before her feet hit the floor. When she'd focused she realized that it wasn't a firecracker, but the sound of gun fire. When her mind caught up she knew it was indeed a gun shot. The sound had been clear. It hadn't come from outside. It had come from inside the house.

"Oh my God. He killed her. No. No. Jonas would never do that. He killed himself," Alex murmured, her voice rising and then sinking to a whisper. She didn't want to face what she had to—seeing Jonas lying in a pool of his own blood. His handsome face unrecognizable.

His eyes dark and lifeless.

She stood in one spot wearing only her gown. She was still standing there when her mind said to her that she had to face this whatever it was. *Where are you Max? Why haven't you come? I don't want to face this alone,* she thought, as she crept slowly and cautiously down the foyer leading to Jonas's room until she reached his door.

Breathlessly she placed her palm against the door and it creaked open. There on the bed next to Jonas, lying in his lap was Brooke. He'd cradled her in his arms, rocking her back and forward, with his hands frantically holding her neck to hold back the blood seeping out. There was so much blood on Jonas, Alex couldn't tell who had been shot.

Alex stared and when she tried to approach Jonas he didn't see her, but she heard him saying, "Don't die. I'll get help. Help is coming. Just hang in there, buddy. Hang in there."

Alex realized that Jonas thought he'd been in combat, and Brooke had been a fallen soldier. When Alex walked close enough to get Jonas's attention, she saw a gun on the floor, and next to the gun, Mark laid stretched out with a bullet wound to the head.

Turning and rushing out of the room to retrieve her phone and call the police, she'd left her phone in her room. Before she could get halfway, the bell rang. She turned in a circle and headed for the front door. She thought maybe someone had heard the shot and called the police. She opened the door and standing there was the police.

"Please. Please come in."

"Are you Mrs. Alexander Blackstone?"

"Yes. Please come in," Alex demanded. "My brother-in-law had a terrible accident."

"We didn't come for that, Mrs. Blackstone. We came to inform you that your husband's plane, the one he'd been flying, crashed in a field not far from here." Alex blinked and stared.

"Did you hear me? Your husband's plane crashed and they think he's dead."

"I need to sit. I can't see. It's going black," Alex said.

"Do you need us to do anything? Call someone?"

"I need you to go in the room to your right. There has been two murders and my brother-in-law didn't kill his wife. He's the one in the room alive."

The two policemen rushed down the hallway and opened the door. Alex heard one officer call for an ambulance, the coroner, forensic, and detectives.

• • • •

WHEN FORENSIC, AND the coroner had left there were only two people who remained in the house after the detectives pulled out of the driveway. It was now dark and ten pm. And they'd questioned Jonas who had been in shock. Throughout the day and night, somewhere Jonas found the strength to understand what had happened to Brooke, however, Alex had asked the policemen not to say anything to Jonas about Max.

"What are we going to do, Alex? The detectives said for us not to leave town. What's Max going to say after this. You know I didn't kill Brooke. I loved her as much as I could love a woman."

Alex wiped the tears away that had pooled in her eyes. She turned to look at Jonas only because she could hear his voice, but she heard very little of what he'd said to her. She stared at Jonas as her eyes wandered around the kitchen. "I have to call the children to see if they're okay. What did I do with my phone? Oh yeah, it's in the room. I don't feel like going there now," her voice was low as if she had no emotions.

"What's wrong, Alex? That's not like you. You never cry. Why are you crying? You didn't know Brooke, and you didn't like her that much, but she was sweet and I know if she had lived, that she'd have made me a great wife."

"There's something you don't know, Jonas." Alex placed her palms on both sides of his face. "There was no time to tell you, the policemen came not because someone called them, because Max was flying one of his planes, not his jet. The plane went down near Miami and they think he's dead."

Jonas mouth parted to say something and he couldn't. It stayed in an open position as if he'd say something but nothing came out. Then he forced words through his parted mouth. "Why us Alex? Tell me why this keep happening to me and you. Tell me something that will make this night go away?"

"I can't. I don't have the answers. All I know is that I have children and I will have to get it together for them." Jonas put his trembling hand over Alex's.

"I'll help you Alex in every way I can. I have to call Brooke's parents and tell them what happened. I don't know if I can face them. I can't call tonight. I need some sleep." Jonas rose from his chair and walked in the direction of the cabinet. There were bottles of liquor still strewn around, and he picked up a bottle and drank it straight.

"Don't do that Jonas. You're going to ruin your life if you start that again."

"I don't have any drugs so this is the next best thing. I can't get through this night without something. I only have you, Alex." Jonas didn't listen to Alex. He put the bottle to his mouth and drank. When he'd had enough, he staggered as he held on to the back of the chair.

"Go to bed, Jonas. You'll probably be able to sleep now. I'm going to stay up."

"Only if you come into the room and watch over me. You can sleep in the bed and I'll sleep on the floor, but I don't want to be away from you. We're all we have now."

Jonas's legs weak, his eyes blurred with tears, stared at Alex until she capitulated and took his hand leading him to bed. He placed his arm around her shoulders, and when they entered the extra bedroom at the back of the house, far away from the crime scene, Jonas fell on the bed taking Alex down with him. He had a tight grip on her shoulder as if he'd fallen into an ocean and he'd latched on to Alex as if she was the last life line before he drowned.

When she couldn't release his grip she lay there and thought of Max and she cried some more. She cried herself to sleep.

When she woke it was because she felt a presence in the dim lit room. "Whose there?" Thoughts swirled around the room. Did she remember to lock the door when the detectives left? No she had not. "Wake up, Jonas, there's someone here."

"Wake up, Jonas," the loud baritone of a man's voice bellowed throughout the room. "Why are you in bed with my wife?"

"Oh my God, it's you, Max. How, when, where?" Alex said, her voice filled with surprise and relief. But Max in shock couldn't know Alex's pain. He didn't see the pain on her face. He didn't hear her call out his name in the night even as she slept next to Jonas with his arms wrapped around her, caging her in, and pulling her to his chest.

"Is this what you do when you think I'm dead, Alex? Sleep with Jonas?" Alex reached for Jonas's powerful arms, and somehow she'd pried herself loose from his grip, and rose to her feet to embrace Max. He stepped back.

"You don't understand, Max?" Alex's voice fragile, crying out for him to hold her. Her arms reaching, hoping he'd realized that she could never be with Jonas, she could never be unfaithful to him, and this was all a terrible misunderstanding.

Max stood over her dressed in a beautiful black suit that had been torn on the sleeves, singed by fire, and smelling of gasoline. His handsome face scarred, his eyes dark as his thoughts of Alex and Jonas.

"Make me understand," Max barked. His voice thundered and Jonas opened his eyes.

Until Next time. Coming soon: Book 8 Black Label

If you haven't read the Blackstone saga, for your entertainment I have placed two bonus books (Book 1 and Book 2) below for your reading pleasure. You can get the first six books in a bundle, or buy them separately.

# The Incredible Mr. Black

By Rachel E Rice

Copyright by Rachel E Rice

Author's Note:
The first three books should be read in order. There are 7 books in this series now. I'm providing 1 bonus book (The Incredible Mr. Blackstone book 1) if you haven't read the Blackstone series, and is reading them for the first time. If you've read these books you can revisit them. You may find something you didn't know about the twins and Alexandre Blackstone. Read below book 1.

## AUTHOR'S NOTE:

You can purchase these books everywhere.

Sign up for a newsletter[1] from Rachel E Rice for chapter reveals, free books, and the latest books before they're published. You can contact me at: rachelerice04@gmail.com Thank you for reading my books. Please leave a review. Enjoy! Blog: http://www.rachel-e-rice.com

---

1.     http://eepurl.com/4uh-b

# The Incredible Mr. Black

## Chapter 1

The worst thing a young woman can do is fall in love, and worse yet is to fall in love with a sexy, handsome, drop dead gorgeous rich man. Because you could find yourself doing things you never would imagine—like letting him handcuff you to his bed, as he makes passionate, sexual, erotic love to you.

Driving into the gated community, shivering from the thought, I stopped to put in the code. The mansion is setting on a lush green manicured grassy hill with a circular driveway. I bring my SL 500 Mercedes to a quick stop and exit it, another present I accepted from the billionaire industrialist, Maximilian Blackstone, or as I call him, Mr. Black.

A young man reaches for my keys. I stiffen my hand. He felt my hand hesitate. "Don't worry miss, we'll take care of your car." It wasn't the car that worried me.

Walking in a daze I'm now at the front door of Pandora's Retreat, a luxurious getaway for the serious bondage and S and M enthusiast. My mind wavering as I count my steps. I can't decide whether I want to do this, whether I want to walk through those double glass doors with the gold plated trim, and spend a week experiencing a world of BDSM.

I've had only one man in my sexual life, and I can't imagine anyone who could match the Incredible Mr. Black, Max as his friends call him.

I tugged the collar of my cream colored silk shirt and lumbered on through the doors. My gaze turned following an attractive woman heading in my direction, where a faint light bounced off her stern face. She stopped to greet me, "Welcome, Ms. Johns. You will find your stay most delightful, and you will discover that we have attended to all your needs, including an apartment for a week's stay." The director, a beautiful golden haired woman of forty, wearing a black fitted dress and high heels, who appeared to enjoy her job, smiled warmly, opening the door of the apartment and handing me the key.

*How did it come to this? Why did I agree to do this?* I wondered ignoring the answer.

Three years ago, I fell in love and the last thing I thought about was being a sex slave to a beautiful exotic looking billionaire who appeared on the outside normal, but by my standards then, there was nothing normal about whippings, ropes, and handcuffs. I guess a few years ago, I would have been considered Vanilla.

I'm here to meet the Master, he's to teach me how to be the perfect Sub and bring me to a higher level of submission. Mr. Black suggested that I was confused, and I didn't know whether I was a Sub or Dom, and he needed a Sub. I knew what I was, he just couldn't handle it. Finally I agreed to his wishes, but I warned him that sending me here could be dangerous for both of us. But deep down inside I was anxious to learn about the real world of bondage, because until now, I had been faking it to understand, and fit into the world of my incredible handsome and sexy, Mr. Black.

*When did this begin?* I asked myself as I prepared my mind and body for what I had come to love. When did I begin to enjoy a man placing me over his knee, whipping my ass, and tying me to his headboard while fucking me senseless?

It started the day I answered an ad in the local newspaper for a terrific job in Montana, never bothering to read the small print.

Today is my first day on the job. I'm suffering from jet lag, incompetence, identity crisis, and a host of other insecurities that a twenty-two year old who has just completed college, with mountains of debt, no friends or family to speak of, and a new job that I need. I found this position in the New York Post: *Wanted, young gregarious go getter to work in sales, she should be intelligent, a college graduate, pretty without being noticeable, comfortable with individuals who are among the 1 percent...* the ad went on and on. I figured I had one of the qualities they advertised, and I packed my bags and headed to Billings, Montana in the middle of ski season.

I wasn't a drop dead gorgeous woman but I had my moments, just average, long auburn curly hair worn in a ponytail most often, oval face, high cheekbones, and large blue eyes. I never trusted my looks as a magnet for men.

And I never got the impression that the company which hired me was more interested in my looks than whether I could do the job.

"Miss Bishop," the manager Joshua said holding my resume and looking over his glasses, "can you work overtime?" That was it. Staring at him as his eyes glanced intermittently at me; I thought he was a great looking guy, with dirty blond hair, barely six feet, and a great body. The kind of body you get from farm work, not spending time in a gym.

They must have been desperate for personnel but you couldn't tell by the beautiful scenery, luxurious accommodations for the staff and guest, all the food you can eat, and the pay was great. I would have paid them to work at Blackstone Ski Lodge.

I soon learned that the altitude was unbearable and on one occasion I almost fainted. My skin stayed dry and I had to keep a supply of Vaseline and Chap Stick in my imitation leather purse. I was constantly licking my lips and batting my eyes because I wasn't use to makeup. One of the hotel guests, an older gentleman, thought I was flirting with him. He was all of seventy. "Get a life," I said.

Shuffling off none too happy, he tried to have me fired but Joshua intervened, and that's why he and I became best buds, besides he let me sleep on his couch because I was afraid to live alone. I'm sure he expected much more, but that was all I had to give. I planned on remaining a virgin until the right man came along. Handsome and rich, but that was just a dream, the problem is it's as easy to fall in love with a rich man as a poor one, but probabilities are that I would never meet a rich handsome man that would even take a look at me and say, "She's the one."

It was the middle of the winter ski season and the hotel was shorthanded, Jacob took his time getting to the counter because he likes his long lunches with the newly hired. He claimed he wanted to do a detailed interview. I knew better but I owed him just for taking a chance on me.

Reaching for my Chap Stick under the counter, I stooped, and when I raised my head, I gazed directly into the eyes of the most gorgeous man I had ever seen. Living in New York, I have seen my share of men. I have seen all races, all nationalities, all ages, gay and straight, and he was just beautiful. A face like none I have ever seen. His wide dark green eyes, a strong jaw, head full of dark curls cut short, thick eyebrows, and he wore a hidden smile or was that a smirk, the kind I had seen on a billboard for a Tom Ford's advertisement for Tom Ford Noir, a fragrance for men.

Yes, Noir, it means Black, how fitting.

He was just different. I felt it throughout my body. My legs tingled, my hands shook, and my mouth opened wide. He was the one. The one I would do anything for, the one I would give up my virginity for in a fast second if only he ask with just a whisper in my ear.

This does not say much about my self-control. I thought I had plenty until I laid eyes on him. "Wow!" His breath-taking sinful face should have been concealed to prevent him from casting a spell on all women who gazed into his green eyes. Those eyes appeared capable of seeing through a woman's dress and straight to her clit.

Gliding into the lodge, he was chatting and laughing but paused when our eyes locked. Stopping in his tracks, there was a moment of silence, and then his gaze wandered around the room and the room filled again with idle chatter.

I knew he was trouble when I scanned his gorgeous face and body. He strutted through a throng of eligible beautiful obscene young men and women with all eyes targeting him. They leaned and whispered, obviously they knew him. Dressed immaculate in a black Giorgio

Armani suit, black and white Prada shirt, and black Gucci loafers, walking with a sort of swagger, leaning as he walked—like a predatory cat, lumbering through the double doors of the Blackstone Ski Lodge in Billings, Montana with an entourage of three handsome men trailing behind his gorgeous firm muscular ass. His jet black curly hair tousled, and windswept, his piercing green eyes begging me to lie down and stay awhile to be his sex slave on call, I thought remembering that moment. I keep playing it over in my mind. "Wow."

This man was trouble for any woman crazy enough to fall in love with him. So, I convinced myself, keep your wits about you, and don't act like a frigging idiot. *It was far too late for that,* I admitted.

Joshua returned just in time. "Sorry Alex, I owe you one."

"Oh that's OK," I said following that handsome fuck's gaze. I heard nothing and saw nothing, I was staring into space, dreaming and heading in the direction of the elevators, trying to get out of the room before I fainted.

I stepped aside to allow the entourage and that man I would die for in the elevator, hesitating, praying the door would close. Too late, he turned around, his face expressive and light with a skillful grin, a disarming smile he uses to great effect. Facing the open door and space that I now occupied, he said, "That's a lovely necklace." His voice deep with perfect English, of prep-schools and elite colleges and universities, seduced me, surprised me, and then the elevator,—closed immediately in my goofy looking face.

My head gave a quick jerk downward to see what he was looking at. I grabbed for my turquoise drop held by a black string, the only piece of jewelry that I owned, and wondered, what is it? Why would a rich handsome fuck like him admire a cheap piece of Indian jewelry?

As I passed the mirror, I noticed that a button had come undone and my breasts were in full view. I now became aware of what he had seen, taking the view in, "not bad," I said admiring my best assets. Thank God I wore my expensive Victoria Secret's bra with black lace trim, that's because I had thrown out all my old comfortable ratty bras; otherwise, I would never show my face again. I didn't feel so bad now, just embarrassed. I hope he didn't think I did that on purpose. I bet woman were hiding around every corner throwing their panties in his direction. I know I would if I had half the chance.

Scrambling to button my shirt, and breathing deep with shame, I put my head down and scurried into the employees' lounge. I thought about him all night. Why did he have to notice me? Why did I have to look like a misfit around all those wonderful looking rich people and why did he have to make me feel so inadequate? Couldn't he just keep that beautiful mouth with those perfect white teeth shut? I said to myself.

Determine to ignore him the next day when he came through the elevator with his entourage, I excused myself, pretending I had to go to the restroom when I saw him moving in the direction of the counter. He didn't send his secretary or one of his body guards, he sauntered up with all the confidence of a rich handsome arrogant thirty-something, and then seeing him, I ducked low and scurried into the back office hiding like a child who had just stole her big sister's lipstick.

When I finally thought it was safe to come out, Freddie, the new hire, looked me up and down with a judgmental scan with his brown eyes. "Mr. Blackstone asked for you."

"Did he tell you what he wanted?" It took a moment to register. "You mean he's the owner of this Lodge and I'm his employee?" I said with a scowl displaying my anger. "I was too busy trying to find an apartment. I didn't have time to do research," I mumbled looking up his room number. *Yes, the Penthouse suite. Why didn't he take the private elevator?*

"People like that don't explain themselves," Freddie said not looking up from the computer, "but he was awfully interested in you."

"What is his problem? Do you think he wants to fire me?" I said, my voice shaky and shrill.

Freddie rolled his shoulders to his ears. "Well, he asked your name and whether you were married and did you have any friends? Quote, boyfriends." Freddie made the signs of quotation marks in the air. "He didn't exactly use those words." Freddie paused as I held my breath. "I told him that I didn't know."

"Why did you say that?" My eyes opened wide.

"Because I don't know and it's none of his business, besides, I don't care how much money he has, he has no right to invade your privacy."

"Let me be the judge of that," I said under my breath, and rolling my eyes.

The next day standing at my desk reading *The Great Gatsby*, a book I never got a chance to read in college because Cliff Notes were easier, I felt eyes measuring me. It was an eerie feeling. When I glanced up he was staring at me with those penetrating deep dark green eyes. He had come from outside and for once he was alone. He just stood looking at me making me so uncomfortable with those jade eyes undressing me, leaving me weak.

My body shook and blood coursed through my veins at an accelerated rate forcing my blood pressure up and my blood sugar down. I felt faint; he appeared to have that effect over me whenever he's near. He opened his mouth and those lips and perfect white teeth sucked out what oxygen was left in my brain. My eyes jutted up to his perfect nose, dark layered eye brows, and then back to his mouth and I began daydreaming about where he could put those lips.

"Hello," he said soft and smooth.

"Yes? Hello." I responded like the idiot I claimed I would never become if I laid eyes on him again.

"Ms. Bishop... I was wondering if... I want... I would like to see you," he said with a sexy English tone to his voice.

"Why?" I leaned forward. "Did you say you want to see me, sir, ah Mr. Black...I mean Mr. Blackstone." I sound incompetent like I had escaped from an asylum.

"Forget it. I'm sorry," he said fading away into the private elevator. I stood staring at the spot where he had asked to see me with my mouth so wide it could have caught a fly if any could survive at this altitude. A man like that asking to see me, did he mean what I think he meant? Me? Alexander Bishop, a girl who had never been anywhere except Brooklyn, well I could count the states, breathing the same air as this rich, handsome, drop dead gorgeous fuck. He looked all of thirty-five, so I rationalized that he was too old, too worldly, and too dangerous for me.

And what did he mean by "wanting to see me?" Was I reading too much in those few words? Joshua says I analyze things to death. But I couldn't understand why a man who is obviously articulate would just say, "I want to see you."

If I was stupid enough to dream that he thought I was attractive or entertain such an idea, all I could do was get hurt. I had no defense. I wasn't worldly, I had one friend, I had no money, and I wasn't that pretty.

What kind of experience did I have to even talk to that world class man? Maybe he was married and I would be one of the many girls he fucked on vacation, but for me it would be a fuck of a lifetime. I may never recover if he puts his rich dick in me. I would be gone, probably turn into a stalker, I thought. So it was better that I get him out of my mind. But I couldn't. He haunted my thoughts, my body, and my clit.

A chill eased up my back caressing my spine straight into the nape of my neck and settling on the roots of my hair. Wow! It was then I knew that I would do anything for him and that was dangerous.

The next day I figured the best way to rid myself of Mr. Black was to try out my new skis, maybe break a leg or something, and have them send me back to Brooklyn with workman's comp. That would help me until I could get another job and get far away from him.

I had lied on my application and stated that I was proficient on the slopes. So they gave me skis and lessons were free to upgrade my skills.

What skills? Bending forward adjusting the skis, I stepped backwards and backed up until I hit a wall or so I thought. Looking through my legs, I saw a pair of skis with two long legs covered in a black ski suit standing behind me. It was Mr. Black's rock hard body. There he stood all six foot two, in a black ski suit and gear, and my ass plastered directly on his hard dick.

He didn't move. His gaze scanned my hair, back, and my ass. By the look in his eyes he appeared to be measuring the split of my butt for something, and I didn't know what? I couldn't straighten up, my finger had gotten stuck, and when I unhinged it and stood, he never moved. He stood on my skis with a wicked smile, and with me not moving an inch I said wryly, "I hope you're enjoying yourself. Take a picture it'll last longer." That's all I could think of.

"Well, Ms. Bishop," he said with a sly smile crossing his inviting lips, "we meet again." I stood up with his body close, where not even a sheet of paper could pass between us, as if we were entwined in intercourse and he had penetrated my ass. He whispered softly in my ear, my butt quivering against his dick, with him getting even closer, if that was possible. He circled my body with his arms and said, "You smell wonderful."

"Thank you, but could you get off of my skis?"

He moved his hand caressing my chin then placing it lower, "Your beautiful neck needs something, a collar," he stated casually passing his fingers from front to the back causing me to shiver, not from the cold but from the heat of his penis penetrating my clothing like lighting. At the time I thought nothing of his comments. Maybe that's what the rich say when they want to make a pass, and I responded in a childish and girlish manner.

"You smell pretty good yourself," was all I could get out and then freezing. I should have asked, *"What the fuck are you doing?"* But I didn't. I should have asked, *"Have you lost your fucking mind?"* But I didn't. I should have asked, *"Do you think I'm that kind of girl? Do you want to fuck me?"* But I didn't.

"I was wondering whether I can see you under different circumstances," he said with a hint of vulnerability dancing in his green eyes, which had softened.

I managed to slightly turn my head. "You are seeing me now, why do you wish to see me? And please get off of my skis." I said coldly trying to cool the heat that was coursing between my thighs.

When I finally moved my skis to turn to face my fears, the obstruction was gone and so was Mr. Blackstone. So here I am again staring into nothingness with only a mountain of snow for company and feeling stupid once more. I swore to myself that if I see him again, I would give him a piece of my mind—how dare he quit so soon. One minute more and I would have caved in and he could have fucked me in my ears if he had a mind to.

I headed down the slope and at the very foot; I tripped, stumbled, rolled, and landed in a large bed of snow with my skis buried. I tried to stand but that was impossible. I knew that I had sprung my ankle. Looking around, I didn't see anyone. I panicked and screamed, "Hello! I need help, I'm hurt!" Before I could yell again, standing in front of me was the extraordinary handsome, Mr. Black.

He rushed over to me, dug me out with a small shovel he carried somewhere, unfastened my skis, and lifted me like a doll. Cradle in his arms, my breath ceased. Gazing into my eyes, he asked, "Are you hurt?"

"It's my ankle." He touched it gently. I screamed not from pain, but desperate wanting his attention.

"You can't take pain, pain can be exciting and satisfying," he said flashing a smile. "You know childbirth is painful and satisfying."

"What did you say?" I always missed his cues.

"I guess we can't have children," he said passing a dark teasing smirk along his mouth while not taking his eyes off me.

His gaze unnerved me. "I can carry you to my cabin it's near. You're so light." I felt incredibly light or I was incredibly stupid. He could be some kind of serial killer, or worse, a man who would make love to me and never see me again. Nevertheless, I felt comfortable in his arms, like I belonged there.

Stopping at a large house built with logs, he lumbered up the stone stairs with me in his arms, to this unbelievable red wood cabin in the middle of snow and mountains. I had never seen a house of that magnitude. It was built on a mountain with boulders as steps. Strong floor to ceiling glass windows surrounded the house giving a panoramic view of everything for miles. The cabin, breathtaking, and it matched the owner—rich, beautiful, strong, and different.

We entered the house and I turned around mystified at the décor. The foyer wide like a museum had numerous gray leather chairs placed facing the windows, large paintings lined the walls. The house stood half on the mountain and half on large pillars the kind you find under bridges. "This place is beautiful."

"You are beautiful," he said making me uncomfortable. Turning around I spied a large roaring fire.

"Oh, I love a fire." He placed me in a large cream leather chair, setting near the huge fireplace, then picking up a log and feeding the fire. It was his favorite chair because it sat alone with a large table near with books setting on it, and a small crystal chest set. He watched deliberately as I acted like a little girl who had never had anything or been anywhere and he was right.

Trying to stand, I wobbled, he rushed to me and knelt looking up at me. "You can't walk on that leg. I will have the doctor here to examine it." His voice commanding and strong.

"What about my job?"

"Joshua can get someone to replace you until you are fit for work. Remember they work for me and so do you, so relax, and let me pamper you." My mind began to work overtime, trying to figure out what it was he was after and why me? He stood, walked away, turned, and smiled and strutted into an area that appeared to be a kitchen. Then he came back moments later with a bottle of wine, two glasses, and a tin of Beluga caviar.

Wrinkling my nose at the caviar, Max looked at me confused. "Is something wrong, Alex?" I love the way the sound of my name dripped from his lips—so authoritative, so masculine. No man had ever called me Alex; they always wanted to feminize Alexander. My parents named me after Alexander the Great, the great conquer.

"Drinking wine is not good for me, I have a low tolerance for wine, and the caviar is from a mammal, it's like eating my own eggs," I said looking at him thinking I said something interesting. But the truth was I had never had caviar. I could tell by his smile and arched eyebrow that I wasn't fooling him.

"Oh you are one of those," he said staring as if he had seen an alien. "After today with your ankle, I thought you needed a drink. And the caviar, I'll get rid of it. I'll have my cook make you something more familiar." He scooped up the silver tray, holding the tin of caviar, with silver matching spoons, and disappeared into the kitchen. Then he returned looking disappointed and vulnerable. "I instructed my chef to make you soup, a sandwich, and a salad, you do eat lettuce?"

"Mr. Blackstone, I'll have the wine…"

He interrupted, "Call me Maximillian or Max." He poured the wine, and I took a sip and before I could finish it someone rang the bell. It was the doctor. He examined me and my ankle, massaged it, gave me some muscle relaxers, and said that I should stay off it for twenty-four hours and I would be good to go. Max didn't leave me. He sat and waited for the doctor to finish examining me. The last thing I remembered was looking into Max's beautiful face.

Waking in the middle of the night to the moon flowing through the picture windows, I worried because I had fallen asleep around a man I didn't know. Was it the wine or did Mr. Black slip something into my drink? No, it was the meds. He didn't have to drug me; I would give myself freely and happily, and he knew it. I felt my clothing. I was wearing a silk white top and nothing else. I felt the bed, now I know what silk black sheets feel like. I smiled. I guess he likes black. Then in the moonlight I saw a tall figure standing with his legs crossed in the doorway, his hand on his hip. "Are you ok?"

"Who undressed me? How did you know my size?" he answered one of my questions.

"Me. We are adults after all," he said inching in my direction.

"We may be adults but you are my employer," I said wincing. "I'll never be able to look at you without feeling uncomfortable."

"Well you will not have to see me again unless you want to." He strutted close to the bed and sat at the corner staring down at me. "Do you find me attractive?"

"What kind of question is that?" *A blind woman would find him attractive just from his voice. Didn't he know how handsome and sexy he is especially in the moonlight?*

"I was taken with you the moment I saw your beautiful face," he said with a secret smile.

*You weren't looking at my face it was my breasts, you sexy fuck.* Was he serious? Maybe he was blind and I hadn't notice. Maybe he had a missing leg or he was impotent and he would seduce anyone he could fool? Why me?

All possibilities crossed my mind, I came to a conclusion,—I didn't care. He leaned over to kiss me. I leaned back away from his full lips. "I don't think we should do this." *I was going but I didn't want to go easy.*

"I won't tell if you don't," he said with a gleeful smile.

"I'm not what you think I am?" I said trying for respectability.

"You are exactly what I think you are?" he said with a twist of his head.

"Some kind of slut you can give wine to and I'll do anything to be near a rich good-looking guy like you."

"So you find me appealing."

"Well, yes in a kind of sexy odd way."

"Now I'm sexy?" he questioned with a soft smile and glowing eyes. He moved closer and leaned in to me. I tried to move away when he draped his muscular arm across my lap and trapped me.

"I didn't quite mean it like that."

"What if I told you that I'm attracted to you?" Mr. Black said, eyes penetrating my glance.

"What if I told you that I'm not attracted to you," I said wanting to take those words back the minute they slipped from my lips.

"Then I'm hurt. Feel my heart, it's broken." Mr. Black took my hand and placed it to his hard chest. I felt his heart beating quickly as he nudged his face closer to my neck. My body responded to his closeness. His hand pushed my hair to the side and he planted kisses on my neck, on my chin, and on my lips.

First a soft kiss, then one on the nape of my neck. He placed his strong manicured hand around my back to brace me, threading his hand through my curly unruly auburn hair and said, "I'm turned on by your lips, which makes me want to..." He didn't finish his thoughts. He strummed his finger over my top lip. *Maybe it was too soon for him to say that he wanted me to wrap my full lips around his hard dick.*

Passing his finger on my bottom lip and letting it linger, his eyes smoldering and dark. Then he took my fingers and placed it in his mouth. I watched as he kissed it and then he closed his eyes and sucked them. I watched in wonder. I felt a tingle move down my breasts and settle on my clit then to my toes. This type of foreplay was new to me. I felt intensely drawn to him like metal drawn to a magnet. It was something sinful about how he kissed my fingers and then his lips found my mouth.

His tongue swirled around and sucked my tongue as long as he sucked my finger. I tried to reciprocate drawing in his tongue, but he was in control and sucked my mouth dry. Determine to seduce me with his foreplay; I was more than determined to allow him.

Lowering his head to my neck, he softly nipped it. The feeling was felt in my folds. His hands grabbed both breasts and his fingers squeezed my nipples until they rose and ached with pleasure. His dark green eyes searched my eyes as he lay over me biting my neck and squeezing my nipples harder. I didn't cry out because surprisingly, I enjoyed the intensity of his love making. His gaze locked on me and he saw in my eyes that I enjoyed every moment of his painful seduction.

"Does pain give you pleasure?" he said meeting my gaze and his fingers tightening on my nipples. *Yes, how did he know? I just found out.*

"Yes, yes, harder," I moaned breathless. His eyes gleaming, he pinched my nipples harder. My breathing intensified.

His head moving down, his short curly locks brushed against my breasts. I threaded my fingers through his dark locks, and with his mouth he sucked each nipple, careful to tug each one in his teeth until they rose and turned red. I gave out a low moan. When I shouted it was with pleasure. He appeared hungry for a body and that body lay in his bed and it was mine.

And I felt as if I had won the lottery. I was a lucky fuck for the day.

The compromise of my beliefs for that beautiful man making a meal out of my breasts, gorging himself until he felt satisfied filled me with pleasure. He took them in his hands, "These are beautiful, I can't get enough of them," he said stroking them forward pinching each nipple as they met his fingers, "and they are mine." A dark gleam settled in his eyes. A penetrating look caused me to pull the straps of the silk top down my hips, leaving the thong, a thin strip up my ass, masquerading as underwear.

He helped pull the top down and looked on me with my breasts heaving up and down. He straddled me as his eyes searched every inch of my body. Then he reached his large hands on both sides of the string and with one jerk, the strings came undone and his gaze lowered and settled on my pubic hair.

"Let it grow, don't shave it again," he demanded. Then sliding down my body slowly, stopping to place a warm kiss on my stomach, his hands parted my legs, and he dropped his magnificent face between my legs. His tongue searched my clit until he found the spot he had been looking for. He caught me by surprise. My legs trembled, but soon relaxed and I opened them wide.

I carelessly draped my legs over his shoulder which excited me as well as him because he clutched them with both hands never coming up for breath.

His head moved with the intensity and the rhythm of his tongue. I wanted to know how it felt to have a man eat me. I had heard about it, but I didn't know it was so pleasurable. His energy was boundless. His hands cupped my breasts and his fingers pinched my nipples as he worked his tongue. He had mastered a rhythm with his lips, tongue, hands, and fingers—the epitome of extreme multi-tasking.

I had my first orgasm and before I could yell I had another one. It was a terrific feeling and I could not contain a scream of pleasure. With a smile on his face, he moved and eased his body up gazing in my eyes. I took his dick into my hands and he looked at me his eyes begging me to do something with it or to it. It was so hard when I placed it in my mouth, lying on my back. I feared that my mouth could not contain it.

He saw the panic in my eyes; I didn't want to do the wrong thing. I took it out, "I've never done this before," I said looking up at Mr. Black.

"I know," he said softly.

How did he know, I asked myself? Now was not the time to analyze.

"I'll teach you. I'll teach you to satisfy me." Those words sound promising. Maybe I wasn't a one night stand after all, but I was certainly his cunt for the day. As he directed me to hold his warm dick in my hand, I clutched it gently. "No you're holding it like you're afraid of it. Tighter."

Finally, I got it. I felt in control as he tilted his head back moaning with pleasure, "Alex, yes, that's what I like. Now suck it hard. I don't want to fill your mouth with my come, I want to fill your pussy. I can't wait."

With little patience, I sucked the head of his penis; up and down my mouth took it in. I wanted to control that dark, handsome, sexy, and titillating love of my life, man of my dreams, fucking trouble, who has ruined me for other men.

Tasting a hint of warm fluid, dropping slow, drip by drip until he pulled his dick from my mouth, and he held it with a painful expression. Then with his strong arms he lifted me up facing him. With his head buried in my breasts, he whispered, "Put it in Alex." I hesitated, my hands quivered at the thought of the pain his hot wet penis would inflict on the walls of my vagina. I guided his hard penis into the mouth of my vagina and stopped. I glared at Mr. Black with panicked eyes.

"You're a virgin, I know. I'll be careful." His mouth locked around my nipple, his long arm reaching, and his fingers finding my folds, sending a current shooting to my toes. He opened my wet folds and inserted a finger, softly another finger, then breaching my wall. Taking his fingers out, he placed them to his nose and inhaled, then inserting them in his mouth on his tongue, and said, "It's your smell that turns me on. That smell tells me no man has been here."

Holding my breath, he plowed the tip of his heavy penis into my vagina, inch by inch, taking more of my opening until he reached a roadblock. Then with a quick thrust he filled my vagina, as if he had heard somewhere that to limit the pain and reach the summit of a mountain, he had to do it quickly.

The nerves of my clit came alive. Opening my mouth to scream, his mouth cupped my mouth and he sucked my tongue in, rendering me speechless as he arched his body deep into my opening. I became use to his incredible hard penis. I took it in easily, it was a good fit. I knew it and he knew it.

Overmatched by his incredible body, his incredible lovemaking, his incredible handsome face, I yield everything to him.

His energy was boundless, "I need more," his glance laying on my body instead of my eyes. I didn't say a word. I was numb from the meds. But I knew what I was doing and where I was going.

He whispered, "I should have been gentle, but I couldn't help myself, your virgin pussy was so sweet and irresistible." He looked like a child declaring that he could not resist a piece of candy.

Mr. Black's face softened and enjoyment and pleasure took hold. I wanted to give him the pleasure of my body where he would never forget me. As he thrust his dick into me once more, I met it with enjoyment, as I tried to find out just what turned on my gorgeous fuck of a man. My finger nails trailed up and down his back until I found that he responded. "Fuck me Alex, never stop. I love you, you're mine, and I'm your first."

*And you will be my only man. I don't want anyone but you. Ever!* I thought.

Leaning his head back his breathing intensified. I worked my hips at each positive expression on his face. His animalistic moans caused me to thrust forward into him and milk his penis up and down with my tight cunt. His body shook violently with pleasure and his come slowly drained into me.

He pulled me close, our eyes met as I lay with my head on his hard muscular arm. I looked around and saw a large moon casting light on his hard chest. He knew all about me, but I knew nothing of him except that I loved him and he said that he loved me. I wanted to believe him.

Turning facing me with his hands between my thighs, "Alex, you look so sexy, I want more of you." He nudged under me and stroked my behind. His gaze covered my body as he fought off sleep. But he wasn't successful and sleep won out. I was too giddy to close my eyes. I just stared at him with his drop dead looks and body; his arm draped across my stomach, I wondered how I had gotten so lucky. Then I realized that I had never been lucky. I turned lying in his arms with my head on his chest, and I remained in a state of ignorant bliss.

Waking to a clear sky and scenery to die for, anxious to take a shower, I attempted to get up, when in walked a burly red headed woman with her hair in a tight bun. "Ms. Bishop, I'm your nurse. Mr. Blackstone instructed me to bath you and not allow you to walk on that ankle," she stated like a drill sergeant.

"Yes, but where is Mr. Blackstone?" I questioned, my eyes searching around for my Mr. Black.

"Mr. Blackstone placed a letter on the night table with instructions for you to follow. He had meetings and then he's flying on to San Francisco."

"Did Mr. Blackstone say anything about returning to Montana?"

"He doesn't share that type of information with me, Ms. Bishop," she said looming over me.

"Of course he doesn't, you are the nurse, not his secretary," I said full of sarcasm, taking my anger out on someone, anyone. I felt used. But that could not be, *"we are all adults,"* Mr. Black had stated.

Glancing at the antique clock on the nightstand, my eyes settled on expensive stationary. The clock banged out nine a.m. Where had the time gone? Last thing I remember, I was getting the fuck of my life, and lying in Max's arms. Now I'm being ordered around by Broom Hilda.

"Ms. Bishop...Ms. Bishop pay attention," she said with a rise in her strong voice.

"Yes, yes, I heard you. You can help me into the shower."

"Then we can go to the fitness room afterwards."

"Whatever you say," I mumbled rolling my eyes. She assisted me; I limped into the shower trying not to put my full weight on my ankle. I followed her directions in a daze and agreed to a massage that almost killed me, but I was fit for the next day. Well maybe my body but my mind was a wreck.

After my shower, Hilda placed a luxurious white robe on the door and I slipped into it. After placing me on the bed, a maid brought in two eggs sunny side up, English muffin, imported strawberry jam, a pot of English tea and milk. Mr. Black knew what I liked for breakfast. I wondered what else he knew. But what did I know of him. For one, he is impossibly handsome, he likes oral sex and he said that he love me. I didn't need to know any more.

I sat for a moment starring at the fancy envelop with his brand on the front. It was written in the most refined cursive writing. My hands shook as I opened the folded page. It was so impersonal, I expected Dear Darling, something romantic, but it read:

*Dear Ms. Bishop,*

*I have had a most interesting and fortuitous night. It is with great pleasure that I make this admission. Never have I been so taken with a woman as with you. Never have I felt as intense as I have with any woman. Our act of lovemaking is embedded in my soul and I can't forget you, nor do I want to allow you to have another man experience the pleasures I have come to enjoy.*

*Therefore, I am making an offer of employment at my head office in San Francisco, California. I assure you that you will not regret your decision. Furthermore, look over the contract that I have enclosed and sign it and present it to my butler. He will see that the document reaches me immediately. Thank you for your time.*

*Mr. Maximillian Blackstone, Esq.*

After reading the letter, the hair on the back of my neck rose. I sat up in the bed murmuring, "I have never been so insulted in my life. What kind of man says to a woman he had a fortuitous night? Yes, it was fortuitous for you Mr. Black. Who would have thought that I would have been so easy to be seduced, fucked within the inch of my life, not me, and probably not him?" I was a captive audience, I rationalized. But who was I kidding; I wanted him so bad that I would have climbed a mountain if he told me. Instead, I let him climb me and plant his flag.

There he was tall dark and silent, but he spoke loud with his body. That was his thing; he could make love to a woman like no other, not that I had any to compare it to, and then put her on the payroll to ensure that he would have endless pussy.

He's not going to get off that easy, I vowed. I know that I had an effect on him and he's trying to hide it from me. You would think he was too old to play games but here he is treating me like a commodity. I took the letter and the contract in my hands, made a ball, and threw it on the floor.

Anxious to get back to work and forget that hot fuck of my life, I needed to sleep away the day. I reached for the muscle relaxers that Dr. Watson or whatever his name had prescribed, and I slept. I got up around midnight and limped out of bed and through the door. Seeing a light, I headed in that direction. Passing a bedroom, I stopped long enough to turn the knob longing to see my tall dark handsome drink of water come to greet me.

A faint light on a desk near a large California King bed provided a substantial view of the room. There were no pictures of naked women or anyone, no mother, brother or sister. I guess he used this room for sleeping and the other for his orgies. My curiosity got the best of me and I wobbled to the bed slowly holding on to the edge until I reached the closet door and opened it.

Someone said you could tell everything about a person by their closet or was it their kitchen. I walked into it and it was larger than a small house. There hung rows and rows of black suits and shoes. And a more white shirts than I could count. There wasn't much color and then I spied an array of silk ties providing a hint of color. He had a large display of cufflinks, gold watches, and a display case of Monte Blanc pens.

His closet revealed nothing, only that he liked black and he was partial to order and he had enough money to collect things. I didn't want to spend my time over analyzing him because I came to the realization that I was out of my class, so, I turned to get the hell out of there when a figure showed in the doorway.

"Can I assist you, Ms. Bishop?"

"I was looking for something to eat and my phone when I passed this room," I said nervous and surprised.

"If you allow me to help you back to your room, the maid will bring you a midnight snack. " My name is Rodger Van Horn. I'm Mr. Blackstone's butler."

Looking up at Rodger, I placed my hand on his shoulder. I limped back to the room looking in his face to determine how he viewed me. He was surprisingly handsome for a man of sixty. He appeared to have all of his whitish blond hair. His face etched with years of sun, and his manners perfect.

"Your belongings are packed for you; if you decide to leave they will be given to you."

After I lay in the bed for a minute, he promptly brought a tray brimming with cold chicken sandwiches and a choice of three beverages—water, beer, and a cola. "If you require some desert, push that button and someone will attend to your needs."

He reached the door and turned, "The house phone is in that drawer," he said pointing to the night stand, "just hit that button and it will appear."

I swallowed the sandwich and washed it down with a bottle of Heineken beer. I had no intentions of staying any longer than I had to. I found the phone and called Joshua."

"Hello."

"Joshua."

"Who is this?"

"It's me. Alex."

"Alex, where the hell are you? I thought something had happen to you because I didn't hear from you and you didn't show for work."

"You have to find the address of Blackstone's home, it's somewhere near the Lodge. It's a large cabin setting atop a mountain. Someone at work must have the address. Come get me when you finish your shift tomorrow."

"Why are you whispering? Did that freak kidnap you? Did he do something to you?"

"Come on Joshua, it's not as dramatic as you think. I'll tell you everything, just come get me."

Sleep didn't come easy, I managed to get a few hours. The next morning I had been under the care of Mr. Black for two days, you would think that he would have called me. I gave him a chance, but he never called not even to check on my leg.

After climbing out of my lover's bed, I was walking normally. I'm sure Broom Hilda was the major cause, plus the muscle relaxer that I used as a sleeping aid to forget Mr. Black. I dressed in my ski suit before the maid entered, "No miss, Mr. Blackstone gave you these clothes. She opened the closet and dresses and suits were lined up, dresses costing thousands of dollars. I glanced at one dress and thought, *when did these get here? Where will I ever wear this?* It was a Herve Leger bandage dress and the price tag had two thousand stamped on it and the next dress was higher until I got sick.

Who does he think I am? He can't buy me. I fell in love with that man and this is how he treats me. I want nothing from him. Not even his love, I declared in a fit of anger. I walked away in silence with not even my dignity, and sat in the chairs waiting for Joshua. No sooner had I sat down when Roger handed me the crumpled letter and contract. "I doubt that you have read this, miss," he stated looking down on me. I never met his gaze.

I took it to be polite and stuffed it into my pocket. He left in the direction of the bedrooms. Joshua's Volvo pulled up, and I stood waving from inside. It was forty degrees and light snow blanketed the roads.

"What's wrong, Alex?" Joshua said with a mixture of concern and anger. With his help I got into his dark gray Volvo, he closed the door, and padded around to the driver's seat and headed the car in the direction of his apartment. A long silence settled on us until I could no longer hide my anger and hurt.

"What did he see in me?" I questioned with tears welling in my eyes.

"A piece of ass," Joshua carelessly stated as if conversing with one of his male buddies.

"Yes, I know, but a girl can dream," I said peering at Joshua who never took his eyes off the snow covered road. "I'm not stupid. I know it was a dream until...until." It became impossible to finish. I sucked in air.

"Until what? Don't keep me on edge. Tell me."

"Until he made love to me and then he left and I haven't heard from him. He left me alone in that mansion with his servants and tried to pay me off with expensive clothes and another job."

"You should have taken them," he said glancing at me with his big brown eyes.

"Then that would make me a..."

"A whore?" he questioned glancing at me taking his eyes off the road.

"Watch what you're doing." I chastised.

"I want nothing from him. You should read that letter he left, and he had the nerves to enclose a contract. I crumpled it and threw it on the floor, but his butler retrieved it and gave it back and I shoved it in my pocket. I'll read it when I am able to stand thinking of him." I laid my head on Joshua's shoulder."

"You know people are whispering about you at work, Alex."

"What are they saying?" I raised my head turning to face Joshua.

"The usually stuff." He paused catching my gaze. "That you threw yourself at that rich cunt. Those are my words. I hate that rich bastard for making you so unhappy."

"I'll be alright as soon as I return to Brooklyn."

"You're not leaving, Alex?"

"I have to go."

"But what will you do for money?"

"Blackstone enterprises gave me a generous package. I was paid fifty thousand dollars."

Joshua hit the brakes and the car jerked and skidded. "Are you crazy," I shouted.

"You were paid fifty thousand dollars for three months. And nothing about that offer rang a bell."

"I had to submit to an extensive background check, have a complete exam by the company's doctors. I needed the money so I signed the contract."

"You're getting fifty thousand dollars for three month's work." He put the car in drive still staring at me.

"I know that was excessive but I told the recruiter that I needed to pay my student loans. I would have agreed to anything."

"It appears you did agree to anything, but what, you didn't read the contract. Where is it?

"I don't know. I have it somewhere." I looked at him with a dumb look and he shook his head.

"What are you saying, Joshua?"

"Why do you think that rich bastard asked about you? He already had you in his cross hairs. He picked you out from a picture and a binder, and you were delivered to him on a platter."

"Do you think I haven't thought of that? But the way you put it, it sounds obscene."

"You were used. Get over it."

"We were both used. I used his money and..." I stopped because I had lost my virginity, my self-respect.

"He has more money than you can spend. He can buy more virgins," Joshua said not taking his eyes off the road. He didn't know that I hated him at that moment for telling me the truth. They always shoot the messenger.

We finally reached his apartment—a row of small buildings with two stories, all with balconies, where you could enjoy the stream running below, and the sun peeking from behind clouds and mountain tops on special occasions.

This was a time I needed some warmth, someone to talk to. I had to try to forget that tall dark handsome drink of water. I fell into the chair and my eyes following the river as it snaked up and down taking pebbles with it. I compared myself to a stream and Max was the ocean. I moved around twisting and turning, heading for the ocean. All rivers flow into oceans.

Anger got the best of me. I made up my mind to quit my job, forget Max and return to Brooklyn. I had to tell Joshua. He walked through the terrace doors carrying a bottle of wine and two glasses. "Here, this will make you feel better."

I took a sip of wine. "I'm leaving for Brooklyn this week."

"Why Alex? You're going to let that bastard run you out of Montana."

"It's beautiful here but I'm a city girl. I wasn't planning on staying long anyway."

"What are you going to do?"

"I paid off my college loans and I plan on racking up a fresh set. I'm going back to school. After that, I'll figure something out."

"But where are you going to live?"

"With the money I saved, and I sublet my apartment. I have no worries but one, well maybe two." I gave Joshua a sheepish grin, and hunched my shoulders. He knew the wine would loosen my lips.

"Well."

"I had unprotected sex."

"Oh no you didn't." Joshua stood up and walked around in a circle more worried than me.

"I was caught up with that handsome gorgeous soft spoken man."

"I'd say it was his handsome gorgeous hard dick."

"Well that too." I tried to make light of it, and managed a small smile.

"I don't think he has a disease, but that was fucking irresponsible on his part. He's fucking thirty-five, an old man." Joshua went on railing about Max's irresponsibility to me.

"It could be something worse."

"What could be worse, Alex?"

"I could be pregnant."

Three years had passed and my life changed. I grew up, no longer a novice or a sex starved idiot.

A year into my master's program, Joshua text me implying he needed a vacation away from Montana. When I didn't answer, he e-mailed me begging for a tour of Manhattan, promising that he would only stay a week. My whole life had been sucked up with school and life, and I needed a break too.

Joshua received a raise and the position of general manager of Blackstone Lodges and Hotels; I guess he felt he had to celebrate. I met him at LaGuardia airport on a Friday evening, and a cab took us to Brooklyn to my apartment. After he settled in and looked around he appeared pleased because it was neat and clean, however, he found the apartment a little too small for his taste, but he was getting use to the idea and the people.

He walked into my room at eight o'clock the next morning and sat on a bench at the foot of my bed.

"Do you always sleep that late?"

"No, but today is Saturday, and I don't plan to get up until eleven." Out of the clear blue sky he dropped this on me.

"Two days after you left, Blackstone came looking for you."

My heart raced as Joshua took his time torturing me. "He asked me questions about you and I didn't tell him where you were. He tried giving me the position I have now, just so I would tell him where you had gone, but I told him I had no idea. Alex, when he didn't find you, he looked lost, and he sat in the bar for hours alone just drinking."

"Not too lost. The next week I read an online San Francisco newspaper of his engagement to a debutant. I see he likes them young and stupid." I peered at Joshua with my heart broken and not wanting an answer to the next question. "Did he marry her?"

"Why are you doing this to yourself? I thought that you never wanted to see him again?"

"Just answer my question, Josh." *I looked in his face begging him to lie to me. Tell me any lie I could stand. Tell me he didn't marry that silly girl. Tell me he would never marry until he found me, and that he said he could not breathe until he laid eyes on me, and when he found me he would go on his knees and beg me for my hand in marriage.*

Joshua only said, "No, he didn't marry her. But..."

"But what?" I said exasperated with the way Joshua tells a story. He draws everything out and then pauses, keeping me on edge.

"Now he's seeing this woman, she's about his age. Thirty-two, very rich in her own right."

"He's nothing but trouble, Alex."

I knew he was trouble, but then so was I. My life had a series of troubling relationships with my parents and the disappointments, I thought staring at my hands.

"Then why did you go to bed with him? You're sensible. You're the most sensible girl I know," Joshua said looking up from behind his Saturday New York Times.

"I couldn't resist his devilish smile, and I couldn't resist him, and besides, I fell in love with him."

"I have something else to tell you. I'm going to work in his office in San Francisco," I said breaking the news.

"What? When?" Joshua said stunned.

"Do you know what you're doing? You're leaving New York to go to San Francisco to languish in that dull climate where the Golden Gate Bridge is the only place to commit suicide. So when he uses you the way he wants and discards your ass after he has plundered it, then you have no choice but to end it all."

"No, I don't know what I'm doing." My gaze searched outside the picture window settling on cars traveling down Ocean Avenue, eventually meeting Joshua's gaze. "He doesn't know what he has unleashed by his actions. He doesn't know who I am. There was an ad and I answered it. His office in Manhattan hired me just like that. I changed my name to protect the innocent and the rest is history."

"I don't know who you are." We locked eyes. "Why are you doing this?"

I thought a minute. "For revenge. Revenge is best served cold," I said getting to my feet.

"You're in school; you need to give yourself a chance. You're too smart for what I see happening to you," Joshua said as he lifted himself from his usual position in front of his computer, taking a few minutes to get a cup of coffee. As he strolled by, he placed a soft tap on my forehead with the sports section of the paper. "You have never had a boyfriend and Mr. Black and Freddie don't count," he continued as if reading my mind and filling in the blank spaces.

"This is a treacherous job market. Just read the business section of the Times." I passed Joshua who by now was enjoying his second cup of Green Mountain Coffee, minus sugar, snatching the paper from his hand, trying to get his attention. "And Freddie does count."

"You know nothing about that company. You know nothing about Mr. Black. What's their business model?"

"Blackstone Enterprises owns hotels. I have a job and that's all I care about."

"You have always been a level headed girl and now you tell me that you are going halfway across the country to work in a business that you don't have a notion of what they do. Well then what are your duties?"

"I'll find out when I get there. I was told that I would be one of Mr. Blackstone's assistants, and I know enough about Mr. Black. He's a man and he has a weakness for virgins."

"To which you are no longer a member of that club."

"Fuck you Joshua."

"When? I've been waiting for you."

"Try getting serious." I continued my analysis of Mr. Black. "His strengths are his weakness. He finds a virgin and then he is on to something else. Look at his dating card, debutants and girls. I wonder what else is lurking in his past."

"Look here. I've just Googled him." Joshua smiled.

I rushed over leaning over Joshua's shoulder reading the headlines: "Maximillian Blackstone one of the most eligible bachelors in the U. S. or the world. And I bet he will stay a bachelor," I said adding commentary. "He's worth billions with money from banking, hotels, minerals, oil, and inheritance. "That's his weakness—all that money, he's young and hot, and I bet he gets up every morning with a hard dick."

Joshua's brow furrowed, "Who are you?"

"Mr. Black's worst nightmare—a scorned young woman, who will exact my revenge from his beautiful ass."

Sinking next to Joshua, staring into oblivion, shaking my head and having second thoughts, "What have I got myself into? Do you think I can do this?" I whispered.

"Didn't I just ask the same thing, remember," Joshua said with a sarcastic smile and a tilt of his head.

Opening my Dell to check my e-mail, there was a reminder in my inbox.

Re: Work Schedule at Blackstone Enterprises

Greetings Ms. Bishop,

Mr. Blackstone expects you on Monday, in his office on time, and dressed appropriate for your first day. If you have a problem reaching your destination, a jet and limo have been made available for your convenience. Contact Blackstone Leer Jets at: 212- 3840478 and reserve your seat from New York to San Francisco. Mr. Blackstone is looking forward to having you as part of our family.

Speechless, I motioned to Joshua, waving my hand feverishly in the air. I couldn't believe what I had just read.

"I'm impressed," Joshua said.

"Is that all you can say?"

"How do you plan on pulling this off?"

Giving Joshua a light smirk, I walked into my tiny closet, taking out a box with a blond wig, then pulling it over my auburn hair and slipping on my brown contacts. "What do you think?"

"Do you think that's going to fool him?" Joshua questioned.

"I don't think he even remembers what I look like."

"Why don't you come back to Montana and marry me. I make a good living." Joshua grabbed my hand and I stole it back.

"But I don't love you. But I do... but not the way you want, Joshua."

"Yes, I want you to fuck me like you fucked Mr. Black and then trail across the country to get even with me."

"Shut up." I got up from the chair and swatted Jacob across his forehead head with the business section of the Times.

"Today is Saturday and you have to be in San Francisco by Monday, and get an apartment."

"Oh shit," I said raising my hand to my mouth. "I forgot about that. I can't pay for an apartment just like that in San Francisco. It's like living in Manhattan, the rent is outrageous. What am I going to do? What was I thinking?"

"Don't ask me."

"I have to get the hell out of Brooklyn before I lose my mind, Joshua. Now help me pack. I didn't realize that I had to be there that soon. I guess I was so excited about the job that I forgot. I have too much on my mind." I said pulling at my hair and biting my fingers, which had turn into nubs because of school and life. "I hate reading the small print."

I walked to my bed in the corner of my studio apartment. Under the bed, I had my belongings in a box—my degree, greeting cards from friends, some photos, a watch with an inscription from my father, and a pearl ring that belonged to my mother.

After pulling a shoe box out, sitting on the bed and rummaging through it, I found a folded paper with several pages. It looked like a contract. It was a contract. This was the first time I had taken a good look at it.

After reading a few lines, I looked up. "Do you believe this?"

"What? What?" Joshua said lifting his head from his computer.

"I can't believe I signed this and didn't read it."

"And you want to be a lawyer? What's in it?" Joshua said studying my expressions, wrestling the paper from my hands.

We both read it aloud.

*Ms. Johns agrees to perform duties as designated by Mr. Blackstone to be decided and expressed on each day that she is employed at his company. If she agrees and signs this contract then she is bound by the stipulations. Once she has signed the contract she cannot be released from it without penalty of law.*

"Well that was short and sweet. He's a man of a few words, and you didn't take time to read this? What's on the next pages?" Joshua turned to the next page. There was a picture of the uniform. It was a picture of a black suit and a white shirt.

"Well, I have that."

"Well you don't. Can't you see that's a Versace suit and a white Carolina Herrera shirt, the shirt alone cost a thousand dollars? If you have time to shop, which you don't and if you have money to buy it, which you don't."

"Shut the fuck up, Joshua, you are so negative. I'll buy a knockoff."

"You don't have money even for a knock off. Look sweetheart, I'm being realistic. You're way over your head."

"I need this job. I have no choice. All I have is a college degree, college debt, and you." I laid my head on his shoulder, and he laid his head on mine. "I'll fake it," I said.

"All I have is you and you are leaving me." Tears welled in our eyes. There was a ding coming from Joshua's computer. He had an e-mail.

"Oh no...I'm going to San Francisco with you to open up this new hotel."

We were dancing around in circles. "Now I can keep my eye on you."

"I don't need a baby sitter," I shot back.

"You need something."

"Yes, some money."

"I have a little. You know there's a rider attached to this contract. Do you want me to read it?"

"No. I don't want to be depressed and I don't want to hear what you have to say today. I'll read it later. I have committed myself already. Knowing more will only make me upset."

"You will never read this until you have to," Joshua said staring me down. "Oh well." And he threw the contract back in my shoe box, saying, "Procrastinator."

# Chapter 4

We stepped off Blackstone's private jet, in cloudy fog ridden San Francisco. A limo driver text Joshua, we quickly found him and we were off to our destination. I tagged along with him. After all he was the executive and I was promised a job editing a newsletter, and writing pieces for Blackstone's online publications, to promote oil drilling.

Stopping at the door of a luxurious apartment with the Golden Gate Bridge as part of the scenery, our bags were handed to the doorman and he quickly placed them in the apartment before we reached the eighth floor. The carpet, lush, and high, lined the Italian marble walkway, glowed throughout the building. Incredible. Joshua's gaze wandered and he said, "I can get use to this." "An apartment, six figure income to manage Blackstone's properties and all because I know you."

"What do you mean?"

"The only reason Blackstone gave me a large salary is because he hopes I will tell him something about you."

"He probably forgot about me. Well, I sure hope he has because it will make it much easier to do what I need to do," I said with a weak heart.

Walking through the apartment; there were two bedrooms, which were perfect. Modern furniture, no antiques. I fell across the bed and could not move and fell asleep because of the time change. I woke the next day and we decided to go for a walk to see the city. We needed some coffee and straggled into the nearest pub which was opened all hours selling Cappuccino, a drink with chocolate, brandy, and steamed milk, served in the mornings, and by night, you could get a good dark beer and a Manhattan.

Plopping down in a booth in the corner of the restaurant, suddenly a pair of green eyes attached to a familiar handsome face turned in our direction. I hit Joshua on the arm. "He's coming this way," I whispered.

"Who?" a reflex action took over and Joshua raised his menu in front of his face.

Before I could leave the booth and tell Joshua that our boss was standing in front of us, I was facing him. "Excuse me, but I think I know you from somewhere." *Yes, you love of my life, you rich handsome fuck, who buried your face between my legs, and left me with the taste of your dick in my mouth, and fucked me every which way but loose. You treated me like a whore; yes, you do know me, you sexy bastard.* I wanted to say all those things, but I didn't.

"I'm sorry, I've never met you." I smiled flicking my pony tail, lowering my eyes, sitting, and slumping into my seat. He never looked at Joshua because Joshua had his head turned to the wall with the menu covering his face.

"I would like to speak to you when you're alone."

"I'm very seldom alone?"

"I see that you're not married."

"And what makes you come to such a hasty conclusion?"

"You're not wearing a wedding ring or engagement ring," he countered.

"Well are you a detective or a serial killer?" He shook his head, tilting it to the side and smiled.

"Neither." His sparkling green eyes glowed, and then he let out a wonderful subdued laugh. I hadn't seen that side of him. He knew how to take a joke. Let's see how he handles the joke I'm getting ready to play on him. "Here's my card," he stated trying to meet my diverted gaze. "I'll be waiting for your call." I looked up. He held the card out staring into my eyes as if he could put me in a trance.

I had been in his trance from the first moment I met him and clearly I still was because I took the card from his hand. He had accomplished what he wanted, turning, he strode back to his booth and out of the door with a man who had been waiting at the bar. No doubt a body guard.

Through the picture window I saw an attendant standing in front of an exotic silver sports car with the door ajar. My Mr. Black, the fuck of my life, my sexual mentor, slipped into it with ease and drove off.

"Did you see that? He not only didn't remember me, he was after another conquest with the same person. He can't remember the women he seduced and screwed." I sat brimming with anger, hitting the spoon on the table, wishing I had slapped his face instead.

"I couldn't see anything but that 2.5 million dollar Bagatti," Joshua noted in awe. He paused giving in to a moment of hero worshiping. "Alex, if you don't do this right you could cost me my position and my job with Blackstone Industries, and I like this job. You will have to assume your other persona and please tell me, I don't need surprises. I have to commit that to memory and all the other bullshit you are planning. I'm a part of this nonsense now."

"It may be nonsense to you but I need to do this. He likes fast cars. And how did you know that car cost 2.5 million? I wonder if he likes fast women," I said passing my finger over my cheek studying the possibilities.

"That car was in the New York Times. Alex, there's talk among the employees that he's into Bondage and S and M. What arc you hoping to accomplish? He could be dangerous. Men with that kind of money and sex habits are dangerous."

"What do you know about BDSM, Josh?"

"About as much as you."

"I need to do this Josh. I want him to hurt like I have."

"If he's into bondage then you will hurt more them him. A powerful rich man is seldom out of control, so watch your ass." Joshua laughed with relish at his own words.

"From my limited knowledge of BDSM, I read that once he penetrated me he could not come back for more. But he did come back again and again in one night, and he bonded with me and tried to erase the bond by staying away."

Joshua listened with interest leaning in to capture every word. "You appear to be serious about that BDSM thing. Are you sure you want to cross that line? Remember when you dig one grave for someone, dig one for yourself," Joshua said staring me down.

"Yes, I'm crossing that line," I stated with lack of reservation. "You know about Alexander Bishop, now it's time for you to get you acquainted with Ms. Rebecca Johns. She's a bleached blond specializing in BDSM. And on her day off she wears tight seductive clothes, where she enjoys receiving and giving pain. I haven't decided if I am the Dom or Sub, but that will come later. Her family lives in Washington State, however, she previously resided in upstate New York, is a college graduate, and was hired by the personnel department in one of Blackstone's companies in New York City. We met on Blackstone's Leer Jet and you invited me to share an apartment with you. You are not privy to my extracurricular activities." Joshua raised an eyebrow. "I'm trying to protect you, my friend."

Rolling his eyes and shaking his head he said, "Anything else I should know? And what do you know about bondage?"

"What I don't know, I can learn."

"You already have a full time job or have you forgotten that."

"Yes, my full time job is getting that handsome beautiful sick fuck to fall passionately in love with Rebecca. I want to drive him mad. I want him to obsess behind me until he loses his mind."

"Be careful what you wish for," Joshua said laughing.

The clock beeped at six a.m. Monday, I dressed early to get a good start, where I can become acclimated to the city. Checking the city map, to my surprise, the main office of Blackstone Enterprises was in walking distance from the apartment.

Dressed in a black knock off designer suit, and a white shirt with cuffs, a string of white pearls, a pair of black designer pumps, and an expensive black Prada purse that cost a fortune, I felt like a million dollars. In a brief case I concealed my black six inch pumps. I set out for my first day on the job with knots in my stomach. Strolling to the glass silver structure with Blackstone emblazon over the entrance, I lumbered through the door. Turning in circles, stopping to look up at the large chandeliers hanging in the lobby, incredible, I thought.

After making a few steps, the elevator opened and out strut my Mr. Black carrying a black brief case and a phone firmly in his hand. He obviously had a meeting because he had on his signature black suit with white shirt and his prep school tie. I looked at his feet and he was without his Gucci loafers. Instead he wore a pair of bespoke black Italian shoes.

When I raised my head he paused, then he turned in my direction, continuing his conversation with his eyes appraising and scanning my body. His expression signaled, where have I seen you and I want to fuck you. The elevator slow, eased to a stop. I stood staring him down. My face and eyes said, whatever you want, I'm here to give it to you.

Discovering I could hide the real me under a blond wig, false eyelashes, makeup, and moderately expensive clothing, set me free. I could be who I wanted. Maybe I wasn't Alex. Maybe I was someone else.

Seducing him with a devilish smile, showing no teeth, watching him breathing hard, turning my back to him facing the elevator, feeling his burning stare, turning around, I flashed a wink and a full smile. By the way he stood in that one spot, I knew he was mine. The elevator came, I stepped in, and his body guard touched his arm. I could see that Mr. Black was annoyed at the closing of the elevator door.

His hungry yearning green eyes spelled danger, but I wouldn't heed the signs and I plowed straight ahead with my plans. When I reached the twenty-six floor which took a second, I got off with my ears ringing and my head swirling.

"Hi, and you are?" I gave my papers to the pretty secretary at the front desk. She glanced up at me lifting her eyebrows and twisting her pretty face with suspicion and with contempt. "Please come with me, Miss Johns." She walked me through another set of doors with a guard sitting at the desk. Waving at him, he allowed us to go on to another section. "This is your office Ms. Johns, your secretary will be in to acquaint you with your duties."

My secretary? Well no one said that I would have a secretary. The young woman about twenty-two, black hair and blue eyes, turned around looking in my eyes, "If you need to speak to Mr. Blackstone, you can relate the message to me, or your secretary. My name is Ms. Corday." And she turned coldly in her high heels and headed in the direction of her desk.

"Hmm. That will be the day," I murmured.

A woman of forty came into my office. She knew her place and she appeared to have no feelings about me or Mr. Black, perhaps she had no inclinations or desires for him, which was not so obvious with the young woman who sat at the welcome desk. She appeared to have had a piece of him and wanted more.

It had taken my secretary the whole day to explain my duties, which were research and editing reports on the various entities of Blackstone Industries. Once I completed each binder, I had to hand it over to my secretary and she would edit it as well. It was a secluded job, not tiring but no contact with others. My lunch was controlled because it was brought in. At four I heard footsteps and someone entering the large office attached to mine. After fifteen minutes, a knock came to the door and without a word Mr. Black strutted into my office.

Sitting behind my desk, head lowered glancing over tomorrow's assignment, I glanced up, and there stood my Mr. Black, so handsome, so exciting, and so fuckable. "Ms. Johns, I am..."

"I know who you are, sir. You are my employer, Mr. Blackstone," I said with my professional voice, trying to determine if he wanted a Dom or Sub. I stood and walked to shake his hand as stern and hard as I could. Not with the wimpy handshake I wanted to give him.

"You have a strong handshake."

"Thank you. I like when a man can appreciate a strong handshake from a woman."

"It shows that she likes to be in charge," he said with a sexy smirk, causing dimples to make a large dent in his cheeks.

*Oh, that told me everything. He wants a Dom, or is he just testing me?*

"I was hoping you would join me for dinner." He threaded his fingers through his tempting curly locks. Remembering the day I threaded my fingers through his hair, gave me a tingle between my legs.

"Do you have a habit of taking your help to dinner?"

"Only if they are as attractive and sexy as you."

"Mr. Blackstone that can be construed as sexual harassment."

"Go ahead sue me. I can afford it." He smiled then it turned into a sly mischievous grin. "I assure you, you will have a better time if you just agree to have dinner with me." *He's a persistent bastard when he wants something. I guess that's why he's a billionaire,* I thought.

"I'm sorry Mr. Blackstone, but I have a previous engagement."

I walked around to my desk to take off my heels and put on my walking shoes. Bending down changing my shoes I heard him say, "Did you read the rider and the fine print on the contract?" He turned and disappeared without saying more. I bit my nails, which didn't have the same effect as biting my real nails. At least he didn't press me further. Who reads the fine print on contracts, I thought. *Not I. Not I.* I heard his office door open and close and I began packing my company's iPad and iPhone.

Closing my door, I headed for the elevators. They finally stopped on the ground level and I rushed for the revolving door. I saw a Midnight Blue Rolls Royce setting in front at the curb with Mr. Black leaning on his door with his legs crossed, wearing a dark blue turtle neck with dark slacks hanging perfectly on his glorious hips held up with an alligator belt, and those Gucci loafers on his feet. He had plans for me and I hadn't thought enough ahead to outwit this shrewd handsome fuck. After all it was my first day, couldn't he give me a break.

"You look tired and hungry Ms. Johns would you like a ride home."

"I live around the corner. I can find my way. Thank you Mr. Blackstone but I have a date." I started walking and he followed me. His driver drove off. The street was a one way and we were headed in the opposite direction.

He paused, then asking, "Do you have a date with a young man?"

"No with an old man. I like them old." I raised my eyebrow and gave him a wink.

"Like me?" he asked stopping me with a slight grasp of my arm.

"No, you're too young." His brow furrowed, he didn't want to continue so he changed the subject.

"You shouldn't walk alone."

I looked up at him and said, "I'm not alone."

He smiled and I saw an ease and warmth brush his strong clean shaven, handsome face. I felt the warmth ease through my body, the way I saw him when he gazed into my eyes and said that he loved me. Was that his usual rap for all the virgins he deflowered? I couldn't have been the only one that he professes love for, but I would like to think that I was.

"A penny for your thoughts, Ms. Johns."

"Only a penny Mr. Blackstone?"

"How about if I make it more and put it in your pay."

"I still wouldn't tell you what I'm thinking. A body needs some privacy, besides you can't bribe me." I glanced up at the building and announced, "I'm home."

"If I remember precisely, this is one of my apartments."

The sign read Blackstone Apartments in LED lights. "One of your hotel managers is my roommate."

"A male or female?"

"A male."

"Is he your lover?"

"I don't think this is an appropriate conversation, and I don't care to explain to you Mr. Blackstone." A smile crossed his face. He was as much surprised as I was at my words.

"Call me Max."

"Well Max, thank you for walking me home." I extended my hand and he pressed his face next to mine and our lips found each other, and there we stood outside kissing like teenagers. A hot kiss seared my lips. His tongue sliced through my mouth and I sucked it in and began sucking it hard. His breathing accelerated and I felt his heart and I knew he was attracted to Rebecca, the way he had been attracted to Alex three years ago.

I felt Mr. Black's hands bring me into his hard muscular body; I felt the flex of his muscular arms pressing me closer and closer. I felt him; all of him rise and pulsate against my warm vagina. I smelled his scent, there's nothing like the smell of Tom Ford's Noir fragrance to make you lose all your inhibitions. I couldn't help myself.

Limp, and a moment from fainting in his arms, I got control of myself. But his hands moved from my waist to my behind. He wasn't surprised that I allowed so much familiarity without protest. He acted as if he expected it.

With one hand behind my back, he whispered in my ear, "I want to smell your pussy. I need that and I need to be your slave."

He took my virginity and taught me about oral sex, now he is preparing me for BDSM. I wonder what next?

From my limited knowledge of BDSM, he was not supposed to kiss me or get personally involved if he is the Dom. He did say he wanted to be my slave. I smiled at the thought.

"I need to go; I'll see you tomorrow, Mr. Blackstone." Prying my body from his arms, I strutted away from him and through the large glass door and didn't turn until I reached the elevators. Swiveling around on my low heels, he was standing looking at me like a sex starved school boy. Then a sly smile crossed his face, he tilted his head to the side, then strode in the direction of his Rolls. The chauffer opened the door and he glided in.

I didn't want him taking the role of gentleman, which he had initiated when first I met him. Then he could do what he wanted and I was left wishing and wanting him to call. This time would be different.

Opening the door to our apartment I couldn't wait to tell Joshua. "Where are you Joshua?" I searched around in his bedroom, in the kitchen, and finally the terrace. He had a glass of wine in his hand and another empty glass waiting for me. "Pour me one. I have something to tell you."

"Do you see that bridge?" He said words slurring. "I'm going to commit suicide if you fuck this up, Alex. I'm getting inquiries already about our relationship."

"Already, I just left Mr. Black," I said surprised by the news and surprised by Joshua's misplaced concerns.

"This morning, at the new hotel, I saw him whispering to someone and then he came over and spoke to me. His voice cold and stern when he asked about you, I mean Rebecca. I can't keep all those names in my head. I thought he was asking about you Alex, the real you, not that blond slut you're pretending to be."

"Well, what happened Joshua? You never tell a straight story."

"He asked if I was fucking you. Just like that. I didn't expect that, especially from a man in his position. What have you done to him? "

"He's a man and he's into me. Things are about to get interesting."

"Alex, do you know that you have a clause in your employment that has something to do with BDSM. You need to know what you're in for." I rolled my eyes, "I don't think you are aware of what is expected from that job."

"I can handle it. What could be wrong with a little dirty talk with your dream man and a little sex? It's not like it's new to me. Don't worry."

"You're in uncharted waters, Alex."

Taking time to read the fine print, I thought nothing of it. He expected to have a little dirty talk and BDSM. I knew a little of BDSM, I Goggled it. Besides, it didn't matter. I would be doing it with the love of my life. I figured that I could talk dirty with Blackstone and I would have the last laugh when I confronted him with the truth.

# Chapter 5

I arrived in my office on Tuesday to find a note setting on my desk under a crystal paper weight. He likes to write these damn notes, I thought.

*Ms. Johns, Please see me in my office at your earliest* convenience. *There is a matter that I would very much like to speak to you about. It needs your prompt attention.*

*Max*

I couldn't imagine what he could possibly have to discuss with me this early in the morning. I would just ignore it. I took the note and balled it up and threw it into an obscenely expensive garbage bin setting near my desk. Plopping down on the white leather chair, swiveling around and around, trying to acclimate myself to the wonderful surroundings and scenery that begs for a second look, I stood, walked to the floor to ceiling window, and leaned on it taking in the landmarks that San Francisco is famous for.

My head turning searching around trying to see Alcatraz, suddenly I remembered that I had to read the fine print on that contract I had signed previously for Blackstone. Reaching for my purse, I found the contract, scanning it I glanced at a paragraph that had me breathless, "Oh my God. Does he expect me to do this?" Putting my finger to my lip, *Isn't this illegal?* I thought.

"Not between consenting adults. Not if I signed this iron clad contract with a disclaimer." I was more than pissed now. I decided to take my time, why should I rush? Now I had an idea of what he expected from his assistants, so I turned on my iPhone only to receive a text message.

• • • •

MONDAY 12, 2013

Rebecca, I need u now. Don't make me beg.

Max

I placed my hand over my mouth to muffle my laugh. "Well I'll give him something to think about. I can't believe he wants dirty talk early in the morning." Then I sent him an answer.

Mr. Blackstone, I'm busy pleasuring myself. My pussy is hot and wet and can't wait for u.

Becky

U shouldn't breach your contract. I warn u I'm a lawyer as well. I should have the opportunity to provide appropriate toys for you. How do you feel about a dildo in Ur cunt and my dick in your ass?

Max

I want the real thing in my pussy and put the dildo in my ass. How do you feel about me sucking your hard cock?

Becky

U R aware a SUB does not initiate that act unless it is requested by the DOM.

Max

U R aware that U can throw away the BDSM manual and let Ur self go. Try eating my pussy for example. I won't tell anyone.

Becky

I know what you need, a light spanking, and my shaft in your ass.

Max

I know what you need, my pussy in your mouth.

Becky

I don't know how I can resist that offer. I'll be in your office in seconds; I hope you are ready for your second day on the job.

Max

I heard a door slam and listened as he informed my secretary that he didn't want to be disturbed. He stood in my office with his hands behind him, where the sound of the click of a lock reverberated making a distinct sound.

His eyes blazed with need. He pulled his expensive alligator belt from his gray slacks and tied it around his neck like a dog collar. It shocked me at first but I tried not to show any expression. After all I had signed the contract stating that I had experience with BDSM and it was among my job description. He said nothing, then pulled his deep maroon colored v neck silk sweater over his head showing his biceps, six packs, and a deep tan. His hard muscles brimming, and when he moved his arms to take off his shoes the muscles in his arms flexed into hard rocks.

He then removed his slacks and underwear, standing naked with his large penis jutting out. "I lay myself bare for you. I've never been taken by a woman as much as I'm taken by you." I didn't want to hear those words; those words were for Alex, not slutty Rebecca. For that I was determined to make him pay. "Get to your knees," I said, as he kneeled with his eyes never leaving me. Finally, I felt my power. *I may get use to this*, I thought.

I couldn't believe that I was commanding this handsome billionaire to do my bidding.

He stayed on his knees looking up at me. I walked from around my desk wearing a pair of six inch black heels with red soles. His eyes followed my feet and I saw his mouth water and his Adam's apple move. Standing in front of him, I asked, "How much do you want me?"

"I want you so much, feel me, I'm just about to come looking at you."

"You will not come until I command you to. What will you do to have me control you?"

"Anything you want?" He said gazing up at me standing over him with my legs opened wide.

I took off my shirt and pranced around his body getting him hot and me hotter. I didn't wear a bra. I bent forward and dropped my nipples in his mouth, "Now suck them." He raised his hand to touch them. "Don't touch them with anything but your mouth," I demanded.

I went to my knees in front of him. "You're not sucking hard enough, next time I'm going to spank you, do you hear me, Mr. Blackstone?"

"I want to be punished. I need to be punished." He confessed.

"Why?" I asked, curious for his answer.

"When I'm in love, I can't handle it. I have too many distractions and I can't devote my attention to the woman I love." I listened but he didn't go further. "I need you now," he said begging for release.

Then I stepped out of my skirt. I came prepared for him. I had on a black garter belt and no panties.

I took my stance in front of his face. "You can't have this," I said pointing to my mound.

"I want it." He followed me around on his knees. "I want that hot cunt." I stepped back and rubbed my clit over his face. I stood over him and he leaned into me swirling his tongue and sucking the rim of my clit. He was hungry like an animal. I wanted to scream, I wanted to hold him and tell him that I was Alex. The pleasure of his head in my pussy brought me to orgasm, and I come in his mouth. His tongue lapped it up like a cat drinking milk.

Moving away from him, I took the end of his belt and led him around, then I reached in my desk to pull out a large black leather belt with spikes. Slowly I teased the belt across his hard tanned buttocks. I wondered where he got that tan because San Francisco had been overcast for a week, Mexico or the islands was my guest. "Do you want a contract?" I asked him.

"Only if it is to keep you exclusively mine. I can give you whatever you want." He looked at me like a high school boy trying to score a girlfriend." *I want you, you handsome fucked up man, can't you see, it's me, Alex,* I thought trying for mental telepathy.

"I can't guarantee that I will be exclusive to you," I said watching his face.

"I can't accept that answer. We'll discuss that later. You know what I want now. Give it to me."

I saw a chill of bumps stand on his body. I hit him with all my might, punishing him for leaving me, and punishing him for opening himself up to Rebecca when I love him with all my being.

He reached for me, his penis was even harder now with his punishment, and he pulled me to my knees facing him. "I want your beautiful ass."

"I can't give my ass to you just like that, "you have to beg me for it."

I hadn't gotten this far in the BDSM manual. Was this part of the Bondage thing? It sound inviting but was I giving too much, would he respect me in the morning? I questioned myself, and the answer came back, this is not about respect. You wanted respect when you were a virgin and he fucked you and left without returning or contacting you. I answered my question.

"I want that sweet ass. I need it."

"Why do you need it?"

"I need all of you. It's so beautiful, you remind me..." His attention faded and then his eyes focused on me on my knees with my back to him. Teasing him. Torturing him.

He grabbed my long blond wig pulling it as he leaned into my ass, sticking his face in and then his tongue. After he had his feast, with me in the same position, and his hands firmly clutching my hips, he stated, "I need all of you because I never want you to leave me. I need this. I need you to be mine in every possible way." I had to ask myself if I wanted to continue.

"Few people understand what it's like being me. I don't sleep until I'm exhausted." Yes, I wanted to continue. I wanted to be with him.

I smiled and pushed my ass into his face. He lifted himself behind me, putting on latex. I felt his fingers rimming the opening to my vagina until he was satisfied, then he reached for his hard dick and slapped my butt with it and with a slap I jumped and he drove his dick into my opening.

The pain was excruciating but pleasurable and I gave a low moan at first and then a trail of moans, "Ohoooooooo." I turned my head and Max was kissing my back as he rode me thrusting his dick in and out of my vagina as he fingered my pussy. "I know I should have taken it easy, but I had no idea that your pussy would be this good," he said kissing my back as an apology. "I love you and that ass," he said stroking it softly. Was this part of sadomasochism, or was he into it all? I began to enjoy that beautiful man fucking me and confessing his sins.

*Woa...this can't be, I'm the one that is being sucked in. I'm in to him too much*, I thought.

"I want you to come on my fingers, I'm going to take my dick out, I'm not ready, and I want to enter your hot ass." I can't resist any part of you. I want all of you. And then I'm going to drop my load in your ass." His appetite covered more than BDSM.

His dirty talk heightened my arousal. He explained everything but when he thrust it in, my ass was tight and I could feel him move inch by inch until it felt as if his dick had reached my throat. The pain was heightened and the pleasure unbelievable. When he drove it further, I come on his fingers. He placed his fingers to his mouth and said, "I like your smell and the taste of you, its intoxicating."

He kept pumping my ass over and over until he groaned with pleasure saying, "I'm empting all my life into your beautiful ass. You will not leave me. Promise me."

His voice became deep and dark, "say it."

"I won't go until you tell me." I had given in to him. He was the Dom now, and I was now the Sub. I had not planned for that. He is good.

Once again I was where I had dream of—in his arms but only for a minute. A small knock and my secretary's voice were heard saying, "Mr. Blackstone, Mr. Blackstone you have to get ready for your hotel's opening it's ten o'clock. We had been at it for two hours. I bet he will sleep well tonight.

"Do you want to come with me?" he said. "I hate those things; I just want to spend the day lying in bed with you, enjoying you. I want to get to know you."

"We need a contract," I said. "We need to determine who the Dom and who is the Sub."

He looked at me long and pensive. "Why can't we come to an agreement now? Can't we reverse roles?"

"I'll think about it. Now you have to go to your opening." I helped him with his clothes. He gazed into my eyes, turned his head to the side and a soft smile dashed across his face. "I'll see you later." He unlocked the door to his office and left, then I heard his shower.

I pushed him out of the door and hid behind it, and ran to my restroom. What a perk, now I know why my office has a shower and a fancy toilet. I took a long shower and sat on the bench letting the hot water caress my legs, standing and turning my ass in the direction of the shower head to calm my anus. I could feel every thrust that Max made. I had to admit that I enjoyed every inch of his hard dick, every inch of his beautiful hard body, and every inch of his hard thrust. I had to admit that I enjoyed him in every way. He has introduced me to a different life. But did I want to venture that far?

I intruded into his life for revenge and now I am enjoying being with him even if I have to accept his life style. I walked out of the shower in a quandary, turned the small flat screen on local news. There was my Mr. Black being interviewed about Blackstone Millennium Hotel Chains. The date was a week ago. The reporter asked about his engagement. Oh shit. Anger could not describe how I felt. I just spent two hours giving everything to this man and he's planning on marrying some rich virgin.

"Well I'll see about that."

He said he didn't discuss his private life, and then flashed those perfect teeth with a tan that made me hot, but I couldn't get past my jealousy. To become a Dom and Sub I had to be aloof, and leave my feelings out of it, I thought. But how could I? "I can't do this," I said.

I got back to work, but I couldn't concentrate. I couldn't wait until four o'clock came. I packed my things and rushed out of the building and headed for the apartment. When I walked in, the doorman greeted me with a smile and, "Nice weather we're having Ms. Johns." How did he know my name? I stepped back and asked, "I didn't know you were aware of my name."

"Yes, Ms. Johns. You have the penthouse apartment." He showed me my picture and name on his computer. Shaking with anger, I headed for Joshua's apartment and found him with his head buried in his iPad. He heard my footsteps and turned looking at me.

"Just leave the key in the Chinese bowl and pick up your key and take a tour of your new apartment."

"What? What is going on?" I questioned.

"You tell me. A group of Blackstone's people came over and moved your things into the penthouse."

"Wait a minute, you let them do that."

"What was I to do Alex? This apartment belongs to Blackstone. I don't have enough money to afford this and to tell you the truth, I like this apartment, and I like this job. So take your high maintenance ass over there and let's see how the other half lives."

We left the apartment to do a tour of the penthouse. "Oh my goodness, I can't accept this." The room was decorated in ultra-modern furniture and the walls were covered with abstract and old masters. I recognized a painting by Miro, priceless. The bedroom was the largest I had ever seen and it contained a California King. This brought back old memories of Montana.

I opened the closet, and rows of suits, shirts, gowns, dresses, and shoes. I was like a child in a candy store—touching everything. Joshua explored the other rooms and found himself in the kitchen.

In the bedroom, I hit a button trying to open the drapes and turned on the lights and a hidden door opened. "What is this?" Cautiously I stumbled into the dark room and found the light switch. I stood with my mouth ajar. Ropes, leather undergarments, a mask, I picked up the ropes, "What the hell am I going to do with this?"

I heard Joshua coming into the bedroom, and I rushed out of the room to cut him off. "Do you believe this, there is only yogurt, nuts, and water. Does he expect you to live on this shit?" He said holding up a bottle of imported water, opening it and drinking it in one gulp.

Leaning into the closet, "holy shit, you hit it big."

"I wouldn't call it that."

"What would you call it?"

"Control. That controlling fuck wants to have his cake and eat it too. I'm going to make his life miserable until he doesn't know what or who he wants."

"Don't make it too miserable, you know I'm in this with you," Joshua said reminding me that there was more at stake than my revenge.

We ordered in, Chinese food, General Tso's Chicken and steamed vegetables for me, and Shrimp with Lobster Sauce. It was the best Chinese food even by New York's standards.

I sent Joshua home happy because the meal was on me.

After a long day of fucking Mr. Black and eating Chinese, I climbed into that huge bed alone. I promptly fell asleep when my work iPhone rang. It was on the table near the bed and I fumbled around trying to find it and pressed the on button.

"Rebecca, I need to see you."

"What time is it? And who is this?"

"This is your Dom." I sat up and looked at the time on my phone. It was two a.m. in the morning.

"Max, what do you want? I have to work tomorrow," I said groggy, clearing my eyes with my hand.

"You know what I want. I can't sleep and you don't have to work if you don't want to."

"I'm coming up. I have something for you."

"No...Don't..." He had already cut me off. I rushed to the bathroom and combed my blond wig stuffing my dark hair under it. I pinned it under the wig, hoping that my dark hair would not peek through. He knew by now that I wasn't a natural blond but once I took off that wig and the eyelashes, he would soon remember who I was. I wasn't ready for any disclosures before I had extracted my revenge from his perfectly formed ass.

# Chapter 6

Hearing the sound of a key opening the door, I glanced in that direction. Staring at me with sexy green eyes, long legs spread and planted firmly, stood Max. I felt my breath hitch. "Mr. Blackstone, what can I do for you this time of night?" Moving closer to me, untying the belt on his light beige trench coat, over his traditional dark silk v neck sweater hugging his shoulders , caressing his beautiful chest, dark slacks massaging his firm ass, loafers to match his pants, and he wore a disarming smile, and a twinkle in his eye.

I concluded that he wanted me as much as I desired him. Max reached into his pocket and held out a folded piece of paper.

"What is it?"

"A contract."

"I told you several times that I couldn't be yours exclusively." He took a step in my direction and I gazed into his eyes, our eyes locked. His look disarmed me and signaled that he had me, and that I would do anything for him. Max's body language signaled that he was far away, focused on something or someone. Maybe that's why he couldn't sleep. Although I represented something that he enjoyed, I was just a piece of property, something he could acquire as he had done everything else in his life. Something he could dominate and oversee like his companies.

Reaching for it, I threw it down on the sofa, never looking at it, or where it landed. I wanted him badly. I could feel it with my throbbing clit.

"It's late and I'm not in the mood." Turning on my heels, he grabbed my arm stopping me in my tracks.

His tone dark, "Let me put you in the mood," he said eyes flaming.

"Mr.—"

"Call me Max. Call me anything but Mr. we've been more intimate than a man and wife."

"I saw the news and a reporter asked about your fiancé." I peered into his eyes then down to those firm pecks and large hands.

"That's what you're breaking my balls over? I'm yours, can't you tell when a man is hot for you." He reached for me and I moved away. "I want you to be the Dom," he swallowed hard. "I'm willing to do anything for you. I only felt this way once before in my life. I can recognize that I need you and I'm willing to give in to you. Maybe we can agree on a power exchange, where we switch. That was the purpose of the contract, and giving me exclusive rights to you."

*Yeah, he's good. He knows how to compromise until he gets what he wants,* I thought. "You haven't answered my question about your fiancé," I said meeting his soft gaze.

"That was nothing; I broke that engagement three years ago because I had met a girl, but she left me and I never saw her again. It's over. You have me exclusively," He said taking off his coat and dropping it on the chair.

"Can we discuss the apartment and clothes?"

"No, it's in the initial contract," *The one I never bothered to read.* He eased his face close, smelling me then kissing my neck.

"I want to discuss that room with the ropes," I said breaking the embrace.

"It's in the contract," he said nibbling on my ear. Pulling the straps on my silk gown with his teeth, and dropping it to the floor, where I was now naked. He grabbed my breasts in his hands, shoved my nipple in his mouth, and sucked it painfully hard until it peaked until it was a bright red.

He moved his tongue around it until it stood hard and he began working on the next breast with both hands and tongue. He stepped back looking at me gasping for breath, his gaze penetrating my skin.

"I need to shower." I admitted.

"I don't want you to. I want to smell you; your natural smell makes me hard. See, and he looked down and my eyes followed. I reached over and unzipped his pants, unhooked the top and they fell at his feet. He stepped out of his pants barefoot and without underwear. He pulled the sweater over his head and dropped it on a chair. Both he and I were staring each other down waiting for who would be the Dom and who would be the Sub.

"Suck my dick, "he commanded, and I went to my knees before I had time to protest. " See, that wasn't so hard," he said clutching my shoulders with his strong hands. It appeared so natural. He stood straight as if commanding soldiers in the army. *I had not signed up for this,* I thought, but I enjoyed placing his hard dick in my mouth and watching his handsome face. I knew from my first lesson what Max wanted. Taking his penis in my hand, rimming the head around my heated lips, I watched his face show his pleasure. He guided it occasionally pulling it out and shoving it in as far as my mouth could take it.

His gorgeous body stood with his chest forward, heaving up and down. His head leaning back and his eyes closed. I had him lost in ecstasy. I suddenly realized that I was in control and although I was performing the acts that he enjoyed and commanded me, he controlled nothing. I felt free to enjoy myself with the love of my life, The Incredible Mr. Black.

Max pulled his dick from my mouth just as my pussy was wet and weeping for more. I wanted to suck him off. He leaned over me and brought me to lie on his twenty thousand dollar rug. He lay across and then I rolled over and sat on top of him rubbing my breasts across his mouth. He had a strange look on his face. "You remind me of someone, that's why I'm so drawn to you."

"Was she a Dom or a Sub?"

"She was Vanilla." His gaze lingered outward. "Now is not the time to discuss her."

"Well then, we need to address the ropes and handcuffs."

"What is there to discuss?"

"I don't think I can play your games. I want more."

"What do you want? Just ask. I'll give it to you. He stated breathless. Do you want a car; I'll send you one tomorrow. I'll buy you a house where ever you want."

"I don't want things. They mean nothing to me."

"Then what do you want?" He said, voice quivering.

"I want your heart." Silence cut the air like a sharp knife cutting paper. He rolled me over, now he was looking down on me assuming the active role.

"I can't give you my heart now. All I know now is that I need your body. My heart..." He rambled and I cut off his statement. I interrupted him because I didn't want him to finish.

He climbed off of me and walked and laid in the bed. I sat on the floor with my back leaning on the bed.

"I guess I asked for that," I admitted. Pain coursed from my head to my feet but I pretended that I wasn't affected."

I had agreed to this exciting, illicit, sordid, tempting, sexual eroticism. I accepted him on his terms because I loved him so much.

When Max didn't respond, I glanced up. He had fallen asleep. I covered him up and climbed in crawling next to him under the silk covers. Sleep didn't come easy, and before I could close my eyes, his long fingers were massaging my clit making it wet.

"You have kept me up the entire night, how am I going to go work. Work from home. I want to continue what we started."

"You barely slept," I said.

Standing and then opening the closet, Max revealed a world into itself, a BDSM room. The room had a padded table, bench, and small bed, with various types of ropes hanging on the wall. I spotted the dildo that Max referred to in his text.

He passed his hands on instruments of punishment, taking time to glare at me with a dark smirk. Raising his brow when touching an anal kit, containing lubes, beads, and a probe.

Picking out handcuffs, he held them in front of me. "Don't worry, they're not for you. Put them on me." Closing the door to the large closet, he laid on the small bed with his hard naked body with his hands in front of him.

I hitched his arms one at a time, first the right wrist, then the left to the head board designed specifically for handcuffs. His gaze never wavered, his eyes were on my bare breasts. He slid his tongue across his lips.

As I clasp the last handcuff I saw his cock rise. "Now I command you to suck me until you feel me dripping, but don't make me come, if you do, then I'm going to spank you each time you allow it to happen. Take off that thong, and put on those high heels lying near the bed."

"Yes, Master." I surprised myself. I didn't know where that came from. I found that I enjoyed the games and I want to be a part of it because I wanted to be with the incredible Mr. Black.

I shoved his hard penis into my mouth and I leaned over him balancing on my hands. I reached for his nicely shaped dick, which fit my hand, mouth, and pussy. "No, use only your mouth, not your hand." Up and down I sucked and moved my tongue to rim and lick the head of his penis. I spied his head lift and fall back, his mouth wide and his breathing intense. I taste his sweet liquid and I knew that his cream would burst into my mouth. I wanted it but he had commanded me not to bring him to orgasm. I peered up at his strong handsome face and my pussy leaked with come at his pleasure.

Carried away with pleasing him, I forgot about his command and I wanted to experience his spanking. His gazed settled on me. "You have forced me to come, Sub. I directed you not to do that, you have disobeyed me, you know what that means." I wiped my mouth and swallowed his sweet cum. "I'll have to spank you. Now release me and get my belt."

"I want you…," I said when Max interrupted.

"You are not supposed to speak to me unless I require it. Now get the belt." I gave him a defiant gaze. "If we are to be together then you have to learn how to be a Sub. I own clubs that can help you learn about my life style because it's apparent that you need lessons. And I will start by spanking you now. Lay across that table on your stomach."

The next day my behind was sore and bruised. After Max spanked my ass he kissed it all over and then rubbed it with ointment to ease the healing. His eyes demonstrated that his heart wasn't into hurting me but I had begun to enjoy the pain which brought exhilaration and pleasure all over and we were caught up in the moment and I let it go too far. He asked for a safe word but I didn't give it. My pain threshold was high. The next morning, he kissed me and my behind and left for work. He had another apartment in San Francisco where he lived another life away from BDSM. He never discussed it with me or brought me there. He was deep into the BDSM life, and he wanted me with him.

I didn't know how long I could follow him. I wanted more from him, I wanted him. Now I'm forced to bring Alex out of hiding if I am to have a chance with Max. It was time to put Rebecca aside and allow Alex to take over.

I scrambled to find his business card, searching through my ridiculously priced designer bag, "Ah there it is." My private iPhone had nine a.m. That's a great time, I know Max's schedule. He's probably in his limousine on his way to a meeting.

The phone rang and Max answered, "Hello."

"Mr. Blackstone...you previously handed me your card and stated that you would wait for my call. Well this is my call."

"I'm sorry but can you refresh my memory."

"I was sitting in a pub with a man and you walked to my table and said that I reminded you of someone. You noted that I was not married and that you wanted to see me."

"Yes...yes, I remember." His voice light and excited showing signs of nervousness, which made me more confident.

"Will you have dinner with me?"

"I'm not sure if I have time tonight."

"You can make time because I will make time for you. I'll have my limo driver pick you up at eight."

"No, I prefer to meet you at the restaurant."

"Very well, I'll have my secretary contact you. You can provide her all the necessary information including your name. I'm sorry but I have another call."

# Chapter 7

E xcited to be myself again, I bought with my own money, a lovely clinging red dress I was dying to wear to meet the man I loved, not as Rebecca, but as Alex. I paired it with black pumps and a black belt. I called Joshua and he agreed to take me in his company car to San Francisco's downtown area.

The restaurant was located in one of Blackstone's hotel's, *how convenient.*

"Alex, you look gorgeous," Joshua said taking my hand turning me in circles and peering at me like a potential pervert, and by the way he surveyed my ass, he probably had a fetish working somewhere.

"You're just saying that Joshua because you want to get into my panties."

"Not so. Well maybe. I just love you for yourself and because you've been a friend."

"Oh, how sweet," I gave him a kiss on his cheek.

He stopped in front of a glass building with LED lighting beaming Blackstone Omni Hotel. *Impressive.* The first thing crossing my mind—Max never brought Rebecca here. Maybe he's ashamed of Rebecca. Maybe he wants to keep that life with her a secret. If that's the case, I will never have that man, especially if I keep up this charade. Wasn't the main idea to exact revenge? I asked myself. Now I'm becoming ambitious. I'm thinking of having him to myself. As Rebecca or Alex? I questioned. Does it matter? I couldn't answer that now because I didn't know the answer.

All my thoughts were ghost that haunted me as I sashayed into the hotel not knowing what to expect. I entered the restaurant and a young woman dressed in a black suit led me into a private room with large booths and tables.

"Mr. Blackstone will be here shortly, will you have a booth or table?"

"A booth would be nice." She held out her hand and I sat in a small private booth.

"Can I bring you a drink?"

"No thank you, not at this time."

No sooner had I sat, when in walked my Mr. Black. He strutted wearing a dark suit and white shirt, and lately hair on his face that made him look incredible, and sensuous. It appeared he took off his tie and was ready to relax. "Alex."

Shocked that he remembered my name, "You remember me."

"I will never forget you, Ms. Bishop," he murmured.

"Where did you go and why did you take yourself from me when I loved you from the time I met you. I still think of you and now you're here. It is fortuitous." He sat close to me and reached for my hand peering into my eyes searching for something and then kissed my hand."

"Why are you looking at me like that?" I said with a crack in my voice and trying to still my trembling hands.

"You look beautiful in that color, it's exciting and seductive. You remind me of someone, but she's nothing like you. You know that you have stolen my heart and made me a wreck for years. How long has it been?"

"Three years," *you beautiful fuck, three years I have been suffering. For three years I have wanted to hear you tell me that you love me,* my thoughts shouted.

"What have you been doing in that time?" *Having your baby, fucking you, and loving you,* my thoughts interrupted. "And what are you doing here?" *Getting my revenge, you beautiful, sexy, intriguing man.*

"I enrolled in graduate school then dropped out when I found a position at a hospital in the Bay area."

"Why don't you work for me at one of my hotels? I hired a friend of yours from Montana."

"Yes. I know. I ran into Joshua in a restaurant one day." I paused searching his eyes. "I was your employee once and it didn't work out…"

"Because you disappeared before I could…"

"Call me and explain why after you fucked me you never called."

"Yes, but you had resigned. I put resources to find you, but you dropped off the grid."

After clearing the air, we laughed, we ordered food, and we drank a lot of wine. "I want you to know where I live when I'm in San Francisco," he said.

I felt lucky that he wanted to show Alex his home and not Rebecca. He took my hand, his staff and guest looked on in awe and envy as we strolled hand and hand to a private elevator. Putting in the key, he never released my hand. The elevator headed straight up to the Presidential Suite. His eyes never left me. He was a perfect gentleman, not the hot horny fuck I had just left, who can't keep his hands off my pussy, and his dick out of my ass.

He was as much a chameleon as I am. He was a different man with Alex and different with Rebecca. With Alex he was soft and vulnerable, but with Rebecca he was tough and domineering. He has a dual personality that's probably why he needed two women. I am his one woman with a dual persona. We are made for each other.

The suite with exquisite contemporary furnishings and abstract paintings housed three large bedrooms and baths, with killer views of San Francisco Bay and the Golden Gate Bridge. One bedroom belonged to his butler and the largest was where he slept, when he could sleep, which wasn't much. I suddenly became nervous. I didn't want to repeat the last mistake I made with him. He still didn't discuss Rebecca so I decided to bring up the subject.

"Do you have a special someone waiting for the Incredible Mr. Blackstone?" I questioned, and searched eyes.

"No one you have to worry about." He sounds so definite that I thought maybe I should worry.

"Mr. Blackstone..."

"Call me Max...I want to marry you," he blurted out.

"Marry me, you have seen me only twice in your life," I said in shock.

"I feel that we have never been apart from each other." *We haven't been apart you sensuous fuck, love of my life, man of my dreams. Your dick has been in my mouth, and your gorgeous face and body have been in dreams from the moment I met you.*

"Before I answer you, you need to get rid of your attachments. And we have plenty to discuss. If by tomorrow you still want to marry me, call me. Here's my card. I dropped the newly minted card on the table. I should be going," I said coldly.

He watched me surprised not knowing what to say, then tilting his head, "I'll see you out, and my driver will take you home."

"No, I can manage; I haven't given you my answer yet. For now I'm an independent woman and I need time to think about you and your offer. " He held me around the waist. One more question, "I was the first. Has another man taste that sweet pussy, and gotten close to that sweet ass?"

Turning facing him, "You know everything about me; don't you know whether I have had other men? You knew I was a virgin, don't you know who I'm sleeping with now? Or are you too preoccupied to bother." I gave him a wink and a sweet smile. He followed me.

"You're exasperating. I wish I could put you over my knee and spank you."

"You may get a chance yet." That was a promise I knew he couldn't resist.

My mind wandered: *Are you blind? You have spanked my ass you handsome fuck. I know what you really want, a Vanilla, and you want Rebecca. You want it all, Mr. Black. You want to use your ropes and whips, leathers, handcuffs, and anal beds on me, but you don't know how to introduce it for fear I will not accept you. It would be easier to marry*

*Rebecca, but that's not what you really want. You want your deflowered virgin too. What are you doing Mr. Black?*

# Chapter 8

On a clear Sunday morning, I pulled out my diary, which was hidden in the back of my closet behind a row of crippling expensive high heel shoes, I will never wear outside of this apartment; it was time to document this.

Sunday, March 1

By this time, I had Max completely confused. He didn't know which woman he wanted, Alex the Vanilla or Rebecca his uncontrollable slutty Dom and sometimes sub. I enjoyed the events unfolding each day until I realized that he would see me as deceptive and manipulative. He chose me because he love and trusted me. He wanted Rebecca because he needed her to cope with his world of stress. How was I to break the news to him without destroying his trust and perhaps having him walk away from both? But then that was the least of my worries.

Monday, March 2

Max is hiding a secret of his own, and it is not just his relationship with Rebecca. He has professed his love for me, yet he is continuing his midnight sexual romps with Rebecca, which has me exhausted and ready to call an end to it. He hasn't said a word about his life of BDSM, even though he asked me to marry him. I conclude that he's planning to continue his erotic life and I'm becoming more entrenched in that life style every minute I spend with him as Rebecca.

Tuesday, March 3

Lately Max has resorted to calling Alex late at night for dirty talk, then he shows up at Rebecca's place to relieve the tension that's smoldering during the day. I haven't seen him at work, but he's prompt in the middle of the night to get his sexual fix. I wonder what he's up to now. As soon as these thoughts left my mind the phone rang. I'm having trouble keeping my identities in order. I can't keep this up much longer, too much time spent as Rebecca when it's obvious that Max wants to keep that life a secret. This has to end soon.

"Hello," I said with a low soft moan.

"Alex, you are turning me on. How long are you going to deny me your body?"

"Until we're married," I said with a silent laugh.

"You're going to kill me, baby." *The only thing that's going to kill you is all that fucking,* I thought.

"Alex, do you have an iPad?" *Now what does he want now. I've concluded that my Mr. Black is a sex addict.*

"Yes, why? I'm in bed, Max." *I hope he doesn't ask to come to Alex's apartment. I've had to rent a room just to have an address in case he has someone watching me, or he wants to pick me up for a date.*

"Can I see you now?"

"No," I said raising my voice. I have to be in work early."

"Turn on the iPad. I want to see your face and body." *Oh that's what you want, you horny handsome sex addict.* I did as he said to keep him away from my small room across town. Now he can go to Rebecca's apartment. "Put your breasts close to the camera, now move the iPad down to my pussy. It's mine isn't it?" He questioned.

"I'm sure by now you know the answer to that question." *He thinks he has two women and two vaginas to crawl into. I can imagine what he'll say when he discovers that his acquisition is somewhat smaller than he thought.*

I heard his breathing, and he said that he had to go and would call tomorrow. It was less than an hour when Mr. Black entered my penthouse apartment with a hard dick.

"I haven't seen you, where have you been, Max?" *I wished I could laugh out loud.*

"Does it matter Rebecca? We're together now," he said in a disinterested murmur.

"I explained Max, that I needed more from you."

"And I said I can't give you what you want." His gaze fell on my diary. I took his hands leading him to the door.

"Then you will have to leave." I saw the panic in his eyes.

"I can't leave, I need you."

"Show me how much you need me." He stripped his clothes from that sexy body, crawled on all fours, then passing his gaze upward, begged me to whip him, and I gladly did as he requested.

"Why am I whipping you?" I asked trailing the leather strap across his back, then giving him a hard whack across his buttocks.

"Because I have been..." but he wouldn't confess that he is going to marry Alex.

"I want to eat you," he confessed.

"Beg me." *Admit you want me, you beautiful sexy fuck.*

"I need to smell you. Let me put my face in your cunt." I stood over him as he sat on his expensive rug and he bent his head back, sticking his tongue in my clit as he held my butt with both hands. Looking up at me, "I can't do without you."

"Why don't you admit that you love me?"

"I do love you, but I'm going to marry someone else because I love her too." *I tried to remain dispassionate and calm, and remember that I was both women and that it didn't make sense to be jealous of myself.* My expression eased and my brow smoothed.

"Why are you with me? Why aren't you with her?"

"She can't satisfy me the way you can. My problem is that you want to dominate me and I want you too, but I need a submissive."

"So she is a Sub and that's why you're marrying her."

"No, she's vanilla."

"And that's what you want?"

"No, I want both."

"You can't have both," I said having a good laugh at Max's expense. This is the moment I lived for—to see him frustrated and confused. I continued with the charade to see where and when it would end.

"Rebecca, if we are to continue our relationship, you will have to learn to be a Sub. I have made plans for you to attend a retreat to master the art of bondage. If we are to continue our relationship, there is more you need to learn about my world."

*This is not what I planned for.* I thought. I'll never be able to carry this out. Maybe I should confess and kick him out. But I can't, I'm afraid of losing my beautiful man.

Max suggested that I needed extensive training because I was getting out of hand. I didn't listen to his commands and was too dominant. He just wanted time to spend with Alex. But he will get a surprise when Alex tells him she will be in Seattle.

After an exhausting night, I woke turning over to see the left side of the bed empty, and a note carefully placed on his pillow.

Rebecca,

I have a meeting and later I have a flight to Colorado for a conference. I will be occupied for two days. I've made arrangements for you to attend Pandora's Retreat. You will discover that it is what you need to ensure that we are on the same page, and that your experience there will bring a fresh approach to our relationship.

Max

I couldn't figure out what I hated most, those stupid notes, or his refusal to tell Rebecca that he loved her.

After a long day at work and now dealing with Max at night, trying to keep track of my phones and my voice as Rebecca, I knew this would end badly. My private phone rang, "Alex, I have a week off, can we get together to discuss our engagement and wedding?"

"Oh, hello Max, I'm sorry but I have to see my parents in Seattle."

"I can send my jet and take you and I can meet your parents."

"No...no... I think I should tell them myself. I'm their only daughter and I know they will ask me all sorts of questions. I'll have you meet them later."

"I miss you. Don't go away from me."

"The way you left me."

"That was cruel, Alex."

"I apologize, Max. I never want to hurt you."

"Is there anything you need to tell me, Alex?" *Yes, I love you so much, and I have a confession to make. But you'll never hear it now my handsome beautiful Mr. Black.*

"When you return, I'll tell you everything Max, we need to be truthful with each other if we are going to have a life together." *I was trying to give him a way out. Give him an opportunity to tell me about Rebecca.*

"Can you meet me at my apartment tomorrow, before you leave?" he said with a low melancholy voice.

"Ok, but I can't stay long."

I rushed home from work, showered, and dressed, asked Josh to drop me off at Max's apartment. We drove in silence; Josh saw a tired body, tired from my dual role of dealings with Max.

"When are you going to tell him that you are Rebecca, Alex?"

"I can't tell him now. I'm going to do it soon. I can't take this anymore, I'm exhausted."

"He parked and glanced my way." I don't know how to tell you this but he has been married."

"He's a good looking man in his thirties, I'm not surprise." But oh was I. I tried not to show my feelings even though I was beyond pissed.

"Well since you aren't affected by this, then maybe you should know that he has been married three times and divorced before he's thirty. Do you want to become his fourth wife?"

I jumped out of the car and didn't say a word, rushing through the door, lumbering to the front desk asking for Mr. Blackstone. The young man pointed to the elevator and a security guard unlocked it. I marched in, and it stopped at the penthouse. I stepped into the beautiful apartment, with the beautiful man standing waiting for me.

"I had dinner brought up." Reaching for my hands he led me to the terrace. "Is this Ok?" He said uncovering the main course.

"Wonderful." Max lifted his gaze behind me and across the Bay and I knew he was thinking of Rebecca.

We ate, danced, and when I thought he wanted to fuck, I said, "My flight is early in the morning, I can't stay." He insisted that his jet fly me there. I refused again. Then he opened a small box, went to his knees, "Will you marry me, Alex?"

My mind was in a whirl, "Alex, Alex, Alex what's wrong?"

"Nothing." I forgot that I was Alex. I was so hot for him and so angry with him, but I couldn't make love to him because he would know everything, and my plan would be shot to hell. I managed to pull myself away, telling Max that a cab was waiting. Visually angry, a raised eyebrow, that he couldn't do something for me, not even have his driver take me home, he stood waiting for an answer.

"Yes, I'll marry you." *Have you lost your mind, Alex? You don't know this man.*

It was the largest yellow diamond engagement ring I had seen. And it was the first yellow diamond I had ever seen. I took control of my emotions, I wanted to say: *oh my God and kiss his manicured hand.* I wanted to say: *fuck me any which way you can,* but I didn't. I wanted to give him a blow job, but I didn't. He placed that rock on my finger and I let him. Smiling inside, I strutted full with confidence to the elevator with him holding on to my hand with dear life.

To his surprise I put my hand on his cock, and gave him a massage reminiscent of Rebecca, and he agreed to a long engagement to get to know each other. Then I left him feeling used not knowing whether he would see me again.

He didn't know who I had become and where I lived. I could disappear and never have to see his rich, sexy, hard to get out of my mind, thrice married fuck, again. But who am I kidding? I fell deeper and deeper in love with him. But I wanted to know why he had been married three times and divorced as many.

I refused the idea of the ropes without trying them. He declared that he couldn't tolerate my behavior. And because of that he's sending me off for a lesson in discipline like I was a child who disobeyed her parents. That's why I'm walking through the doors of Pandora's Retreat, to learn what's expected of a Sub.

Entering the room, I glance around and there are tables, chairs, and instruments to cause pain and pleasure.

I have accepted Mr. Black's world. By sending me here, he's not planning on leaving Rebecca to be true to me. The Dom came through the door. Immediately I felt a connection between us, it was eerie. I didn't know why my heart raced and I became eager anticipating sexual arousal by this gorgeous man. Was it his drop dead body that made me hot, wet, and confused? Or that mask that concealed nothing not even those green eyes. Now I want to experience what I had denied—an attraction to sadomasochism, kinky sex, and bondage. He walked like Max and his body was the image of Max.

It is Max, I thought.

Oh this is getting good. I'll go along with him and teach his beautiful possessive ass a lesson. He thinks that he can fool me with those leather pants. It just makes him hot and glamorous.

"Mr. Blackstone, the company has done a complete background check on Ms. Johns and Ms. Bishop," the head of security stated carrying his iPad. Max leaped from his chair and walked around his desk to view the information. "I can send the information to your computer."

"Yes, please, but I want to hear this now." Max glanced with a raised eyebrow and clutching the end of his desk. "The abbreviated version. Now," Max demanded. The chief of security, dressed in his perfectly ironed black suit and white shirt and striped tie, began reading.

"The two women are one and the same. Ms. Johns formally known as Ms. Bishop have been working as your assistant under the name Rebecca Johns." He paused to look up at Max's furrowed brow. "Ms. Bishop first worked for your company three years ago, after leaving, she returned to Brooklyn where she gave birth to a son nine months later and..."

"Wait a minute. Did you say a child?"

"Yes sir, a boy. I was just getting to that. She didn't identify the father but sent her son to live with her parents in Seattle, Washington. She has several degrees and..."

"Stop right there, I will read the rest later because I have an appointment."

Max asked to be left alone. He found his chair behind his desk and sank into it. Turning and staring out of the floor to ceiling windows, he called his chauffeur requesting his car be made ready and waiting. His heart skipped in his chest and the sound rang loud. He placed his hand to his chest as if to push it back to silence it.

He rushed to put on his jacket. How could he allow this to happen? What was Alex thinking? "I'm a father." He shouted. How could he put her through this? He smiled to think about how she had fooled him. Why didn't he know? Max went over the first time he met Alex and Rebecca. He had been too busy with work, dealing with his brother and trying to juggle Rebecca and Alex to notice. But wait, they did smell the same, he remembered. Was he too involved in his own deceptions, his own pleasures, his own problems, to even know that he had bed the same woman?

What else had he overlooked? He never looked beyond the blond wig and eyelashes.

"I'm going to spank her when I see her," he whispered as he headed for the elevators. When he reached the elevators his staff looked on curious, he turned and shouted, "I'm a father, and I have a son." He stopped in his tracks. It's because of him that she's heading for Pandora's

Retreat. He felt that he would be sorry if he didn't make it there in time. He had to stop Alex from meeting the Master.

"My Alex would never allow a stranger to touch her. She's so young, everything is a game to her, he murmured.

If he didn't make it in time, they would both regret their decisions. But he most of all, he could lose her. He truly loved Alex and Rebecca, one of the perks of marrying Alex. A slight smile crossed his lips.

He desired Alex because she is what he needs to complete his life—a woman he's sexually attracted to, a woman who knows what she wants and goes after it. And she had his child. This is what he needs to make him happy and diminish the stress that's running rampant through his life.

Max wants Alex to himself, and so far no one has touched her but him, and she is the mother of his child. He knows that that world of BDSM is seductive, and once she becomes entrenched in it, she may seek out others that will provide what she needs and he will have been responsible.

In a daze he didn't remember exiting his building and entering his black limo, or greeting his chauffer.

"Faster... I need you to drive faster," a terrified Max shouted. His driver knew that it was impossible to go faster because of the traffic. He had to travel out of San Francisco and across the Bay Bridge into the Berkley Hills.

"I don't know why you can't pass that car," Max said but the driver didn't hear him. "Why would Alex play such a dangerous game with me?" But Max was glad she had because he got to know the real Alex.

Alex signed in and was taken to a large room. A man wearing nothing but tight leather jeans and a black leather mask greeted her. His chest, impressive, and at a glance his body could double for Maximilian. Alex felt an immediate attraction to him, her breathing intensified she felt heat settle low in her clit.

She relaxed and displayed the most enticing worldly smile. He marched around her, "Your cloths are acceptable for now, but there need to be more flesh showing. Take off your top. My cock needs to be aroused immediately. Alex hurried and loosened the leather top and it fell to the floor and her full breasts felt the chill and heat in the room. Her nipples rose from arousal of seeing the man she thought was Max relaxed in tight leather jeans.

She had crossed over to Max's world and she wanted to please him and perhaps have a good laugh when he revealed that he was the Master. How funny would that be?

"We will begin with the ropes. Lay on the table on your stomach."

Alex hesitated. "Did you hear me?"

"Yes, master but..."

"You shouldn't question what I say. Because you are new to this, the first day I will take it slow with you. Maybe we should try something different. I will just tie your wrists and legs and if you want to continue shake your head. You should think of a safe word because tomorrow's sessions will be more intense."

"My safe word is Black."

"Good. Now we can begin."

Alex lay on the table, somehow she felt relaxed. His voice soothing, but commanding, which seduced her and sent chills to her clit. She would experience it all in this week and she would be with the man she loved. What could be better? She thought. However, a feeling of exhilaration and trepidation took hold of her. But what could be wrong if the love of her life sanctioned it and wanted to take her higher. She forgot that she was Rebecca and Max would never expose Alex to this world. She became jealous of Alex.

"Now I will give you a series of commands that you will follow."

Alex lowered her eyelids and faced the wall lying flat on her stomach. "Place your hands behind your back." Alex did as she was commanded. The Master tied her wrist and then moving down the length of the table, reached for her legs stroking them softly up and down to her butt, and down again, and tied them. "You're doing great," he said walking around her naked body surveying her ass. Trailing his finger from the nape of her neck, he moved it down to her split, his finger lingering on each buttock, then swirling it around the rim of her anus.

Chills rose on her skin.

"Now I'm going to continue with the ropes. I'm going to bound you where your breasts are exposed, and the ropes will make a figure eight. This is done because I want to experiment with your breasts and I don't want you to be able to move," The Master said licking his dry lips.

He strutted in his tight jeans, and pulled out two clamps from a drawer. "I will put these on your nipples, and if you have pain that you can't endure then use your safe word." He walked to the side of the table and gently cupped her left breast and placed the clamp on her nipple. Alex felt excitement course down her breasts and land on her clit. He placed his hand between her legs and put his finger in her opening and when he pulled it out, it was wet.

"You are a good student. I can tell you are enjoying being bound, and I see you can take a lot of pain. You are my best pupil," he said with his eyes sparkling. "I know you can handle whatever level I take you to," He said smiling, as he snapped the clamp on Alex's right nipple. Still she did not cry out or give her safe word. He placed his finger in her clit and felt a vibration and he knew she was coming.

"You naughty girl, you are coming, and I didn't command you. I think I should punish you."

Confident that his pupil would make a good Sub, he brought out a leather whip. He wanted to test her level of pain. Trailing it from her back and then striking her butt, "Whack, whack, whack," and still she didn't cry out. "How do you feel?"

"I can take more, Master."

"Can you take this?" He shoved a butt plug up her ass and still she never winced.

"Do you know what Top means?"

"Yes, Master. You are taking the active role."

"And you are…"

"The Bottom," Alex stated.

"Precisely. And if you are a good girl I will allow you to switch. You can be the Dom and I will be the Sub tomorrow at our next session."

Alex found that she became more attracted to the man she thought was Max. It was something about him. She had never seen him relaxed before. He was carefree and fun.

She had become attracted to the handsome man under the mask with his curly dark hair, green eyes, and all six-feet-two of maleness.

His voice smooth and seductive, when he spoke she wanted to lay on that padded table and let him have his way with her again and again.

"I know this is irregular, but I'm attracted to you more than I care to admit. I would like to penetrate your ass. That's my weakness. That's my fetish. It's something about you that I feel that I have to have it."

"You are the Master," Alex stated wanting him to breach her ass as much as he wanted it.

"I'm going to take the plug out and then if you have discomfort use your safe word." He untied the ropes as quickly as he had bound her with them.

The Master said, "Get on all fours. I want to look on you for a few minutes." He stood breathing hard. Alex heard him inhale and exhale.

Alex took a deep breath. "Master, I'm having second thoughts," she said still on all fours and completely naked except for the leather studded necklace she placed on her neck for a fashion statement. She thought it would make her appear more knowledgeable about BDSM.

"I understand your apprehension," The Master stated in a cool soothing voice. "Maybe I was too rough on you," he said rubbing her ass with his strong hands. He stroked her butt, kissed it, calming her, seducing her, and when she lifted her butt, he grabbed his hard penis holding it, he place latex over his large penis, as he took a second look at her inviting ass and prepared to mount her...

The door burst open, "Stop it, Jonas. Don't go any further," Maximilian shouted. Alex surprised and confused reached for a robe.

"What's the meaning of this? No one is allowed in here when I'm working," Jonas questioned Max.

"You were doing more than working. You were not to enter her anus or her vagina."

"He did not enter me, Max."

"I know my brother, and if I had not arrived in time he would have you."

"Your brother?" Alex questioned with her voice reaching a crescendo. How dare you allow your brother to...?"

"And are you Alex or Rebecca?"

"This is the woman you almost lost your mind over after she ran away from you?" Jonas Blackstone said laughing hysterically, while hitting Max on his back. I guess the laugh is on you big brother."

"Come on Alex we are leaving now. I'm not letting you out of my sight." Max hitched his hand under Alex's arm and led her down the corridor. Jonas peeped out of the room and yelled, "Am I invited to the wedding?" Max didn't turn around he just flipped Jonas the finger behind his back.

"Max, I will never forgive you for this." Alex headed in the direction of the small apartment.

"Don't worry about your clothes, take the robe and leave your car, someone will drive it to our apartment, and we're getting married. You're mine." He glanced at her waiting for her answer.

"Yes Master, but I want to be courted first."

"You're going to have to teach me."

"Do you mean that you never courted a woman?"

"Never."

"Do you have something to tell me Alex?"

"I think you already know by the way you are looking at me. You know everything now about me. Our child…

"Tell me everything about my son and then we are going into our room and I'm going to spank that lovely ass," he said arching his eye brow.

"Max do you have something to tell me?" He stopped and peered at me with dark hooded eyes. "I have a confession to make and there are some things you need to know."

"Do you mean there is more besides you having a twin?"

"Not exactly what you think. I hope you will still want to marry me." Alex felt that she knew what she needed and that Max loved her even after the deception.

"After you reveal your deep dark secrets, then you're going to wear this collar and I'm going to put on my leather bikini and take out that whip." She paused glancing at him. "You will sleep for a week," she said letting out a chuckle.

Stepping into the limo, Alex unzipped Max's pants, then looking up at Max, he hit a button, and the partition rose, cutting them off from the world.

Their gaze locked, she leaned forward, and he caressed her hair as she rolled his dick around the rim of her mouth. Max leaned his head forward and stated, "That's why I love you. You are spontaneous and you know what I need."

"I want you to try to forget everything and everybody," Alex said stroking the head of his dick. Max's head feathered back and he closed his eyes and her mouth curled around his hard aroused penis. She felt his pulse of life vibrate in her mouth. Her head bobbing up and down on his hard cock, she stole a look at his beautiful face. Peace had settled in to the small lines etched near his eyes. Alex's gaze lost on his face, wandered down and settled on the evening paper. She didn't know why it caught her gaze, maybe it was the headlines:

Fiancée of the Notorious Billionaire Industrialist Maximilian Blackstone found Strangled.

The End

Temptation in Black

Book 2 Blackstone Series

Copyright 2015 by Rachel E. Rice

A**uthor's Note:**
   The first three books should be read in order.

1. The Incredible Mr. Black
2. Temptation In Black
3. Submission To Black
4. Black Tie Affair
5. Mourning Becomes Black
6. Fade To Black
7. Back To Black
8. Black Label coming soon!

You can purchase these books everywhere eBooks are sold. Prologue of book 2 below.

Sign up for a newsletter[1] from Rachel E Rice for chapter reveals, free books, and the latest books before they are published. You can contact me at: rachelerice04@gmail.com Thank you for reading my books. Please leave a review. Enjoy! Blog: http://www.rachel-e-rice.com

---

1.   http://eepurl.com/4uh-b

# Prologue

Alex read the yearning in Max's handsome face, which was awash with dangerous contradictions. His smoldering eyes sent electrical waves caressing her body. She felt the heat rise from within and settle deep in her clit. He needed her mouth. He needed to disappear into Alex. He needed to disappear into her body. Her mouth was the conduit where all his tension flowed, but until she found out the truth about the dead girl, she had to keep him calm, and the best way she knew was to give him the pleasure he craved.

Alex's lush eyelashes lifted. She gazed on Max's open shirt, which revealed his hard, rippling abs. Her hand caressed each one. He was her guilty pleasure—her temptation in black.

She reached and held Max's hard penis in her hands, and a smile crept across his face. His thumb slid over her lips. Knowing how his body would react, she teased it by circling the head of his shaft around her open mouth. Blowing soft, warm air, she watched Max's eyes flutter and close. With a slight parting of his lips, a wisp of air shuttled out. "Yes, yes, you know what to do to me," he whispered. Her hand moved the length of his hard cock, up and down.

Alex opened her mouth wide. Guiding his penis in slowly, she sucked it, harder. His eyes remained shut. He was in a world of his own—blissful sexual peace. He mumbled something low and Alex couldn't hear his words clearly. She thought he whispered, "I love you, I love you...Rebecca," or was it Alex? She felt his arousal; his penis was increasing in her mouth. It was getting longer and wider. He pushed his hips into her, and she reached for him and sank her hands into his hard ass. She felt it flex and tighten. Leaning her face over him, she felt as if she couldn't take another inch when to her surprise the muscles in her throat relaxed.

With her hands massaging his buttocks and her mouth clamped firmly around his penis, Alex sucked harder, driving him into a world of pleasure and heights of ecstasy. She was taking everything from him, and tried as he may, he couldn't resist her. She had taken control of his sexual life and without her, what would he do? No woman had ever satisfied him as completely as Alex.

The thought of having another woman besides Alex—he refused to entertain the idea.

Alex tasted a hint of warm come on her tongue, and she knew that he was over the edge. She was controlling this man who was used to being in charge. She was now the puppet master and it felt great with a man like him—a handsome sexual animal.

Drawing her mouth in with one hard suck, his body contorted, and Max let out a primal sound of erotic ecstasy and his eyes opened like the shutter of a camera. His gaze locked on her. Warm fluid flowed into Alex's mouth. He breathed in and out. His chest moved up and down. She met his gaze, and her eyes closed, and with a slight raise of her head, she swallowed his come.

It was a challenging gesture. And he knew it. He was aware that she was in control.

Alex's eyes opened, holding his glance. Her body was excited from the pleasure she had given Max. With eyes wide and his breathing heavy, Max said, "Damn, Alex, you took my orgasm from me when I wasn't ready. This has never happened to me before." A mischievous grin escaped from Alex—eyes sparkling with warmth and achievement, enjoying her power.

She thought, *there is always the first time for everything, my dangerous, handsome Mr. Black.*

# Don't miss out!

Visit the website below and you can sign up to receive emails whenever Rachel E Rice publishes a new book. There's no charge and no obligation.

https://books2read.com/r/B-A-ASU-RPNDB

**BOOKS 2 READ**

Connecting independent readers to independent writers.

Did you love *Back to Black*? Then you should read *The Incredible Mr. Black Box Set*[1] by Rachel E Rice!

[2]

Maximillian Blackstone's gaze washed over Alex's body, leaving him inflexible, excited, and with an image of him devouring her until she becomes weak and submissive. He desired nothing more than to spend his days inside her sexy alluring body, satisfying himself with erotic pleasures, which only a man with a fixated obsession, and fascinations with S&M and Bondage can understand and enjoy.

**Alex**

"Yes, he is the most indecent, delicious, handsome, arrogant man; his blue eyes circle with dark lashes and when he stares at me, a hot wave of desire surrounds me, covering me, taking me away into his

---

1. https://books2read.com/u/mv67Xm

2. https://books2read.com/u/mv67Xm

arms, where I forget I'm married to Maximilian Blackstone, the love of my life."

**Max**

"Alex is all I've ever wanted in life, but my nature is stronger than her love, and it is calling me to the lifestyle I left behind."

**Robert**

"I envy Maximilian Blackstone because he has a woman I need and I will do anything to make her mine."

Read more at www.rachel-e-rice.com.

# Also by Rachel E Rice

**Blackstone**
The Incredible Mr. Black
Blackstone Complete 10 Books Dark Romance Series
Temptation In Black
Blackstone Series 4 Books Box Set
Submission To Black
Black Tie Affair
The Incredible Mr. Black Box Set
Mourning Becomes Black
Fade To Black
Back to Black
Black Tide
Black Swan
Blackout
Blackstone Series 6 Books Box Set

**I Am The Night**
I Am The Night

**Insatiable**

Insatiable: The Lone Werewolf finds his mate
Insatiable: A Werewolf's Hunger
Insatiable: A Werewolf's Wedding
Insatiable: The Werewolves' Challenge
Hunter's Moon
Moon Tide
Moon Rapture

**Insatiable Werewolf Series**
A Bride For A Werewolf: The Beginning
Thorn in Moonscape
Insatiable: Damon in Moonscape
A Werewolf's Passion
Moonscape Box Set

**Night**
I Am First Night
I Am Last Night

**Obsession**
Obsession: Warm Bodies,Cold Hearts
Naked Obsession
Burning Obsession

**Seduction**
Seduced By An Earl

**The Captain**
The Captain and The Virgin


**The Soul of A Vampire**
Soul of A Vampire
Soul of A Vampire Book 2
Soul of A Vampire Book 3


**To kill a vampire**
To Kill a Vampire
To Kill A Vampire
To Kill A Vampire


**Standalone**
Finding Summer
One Desire
Insatiable Box Set: Books 1-4
Hunter's Moon Box Set
Hunter's Moon Insatiable Series
Insatiable: Tracker #8
Soul of A Vampire Box Set
The Complete Insatiable Werewolf Bundle
The Complete Insatiable Werewolf Bundle
I Am The Night Box Set
A Vampire Bundle
A Vampire Bundle

I Am The Night Box Set
To Kill A Vampire Boxset
To kill A Vampire Boxset
A Complete Vampire Bundle


Watch for more at www.rachel-e-rice.com.

# About the Author

Rachel E. Rice enjoys writing in different genres. As an Indie author she explores genres to find her voice. She has written contemporary romance, erotic romance, new adult, historical and science fiction.

When she's not writing she is reading poetry. She has a BA and is a member of Romance Writers of America.

Read more at www.rachel-e-rice.com.

www.ingramcontent.com/pod-product-compliance
Lightning Source LLC
Chambersburg PA
CBHW050333160726
48002CB00001B/292